The Christmas Layover

CHERYL BARTON

It's Christmas in July!

Who says a Christmas romance novel can only be released during the winter months? No one, that's for sure.

Everyone has a past, some good some bad, perhaps even pretty awful. That doesn't mean they don't deserve a second chance at love. I believe in love especially when hearts and spirits connect before mind and body. That's exactly what happened between investigative journalist, Danica Green and self-made millionaire and powerhouse stock market trader, Edrick Stone.

Danica is picked to go on an assignment to dive into Edrick's life to see if his business savvy is on the up-and-up or if he's running a Ponzi scheme. She made a mistake in her past when it came to boosting her own career. She knows that this story could thrust her into the perfect job that she's always dreamed of.

Five years after the death of his wife and son, Edrick instantly falls for a woman he feels connected to on a level he had not experienced since he met his wife, the woman he thought he would have forever with. A chance meeting and a flight layover could provide him with the opportunity to find out if he believes in love a second time around.

Keep an open mind as you dive into Danica and Edrick's story. Not all love is found on a straight line. There are times when there are bumps in the road, but the end result is still love at last.

Also by Cheryl Barton
www.cherylbarton.net
www.crbarton.com
Upcoming Novels

The Sullivans of Montana
Home for Thanksgiving, Book 1
The Way You Love Me, Book 2
On the Right Track, Book 3
Three's a Crowd, Book 4 – Preorder available

Sister Act
An Unexpected Destiny, Book 1
For You I Will, Book 2 - Preorder available
More Than Friends, Book 3

Game Changers
On the Lam, Book 1

Bachelor Series
Bachelor Not for Sale
A Designed Affair
A Perfect Combination
Love at Last

A Lovers' Heart Series
Heartthrob
Heartbeat
Heartbreaker

Brothers of Chi-Town Series
I Can't Let Go, Book 1
Swagger and Baggage, Book 2
Claiming His Child, Book 3
Always Bet on Black, Book 4
It Takes Two to Tangle, Book 5
Crashing into Love, Book 6
Leaks, Lies, Lust and Love, Book 7

Prologue

From: Hailey.Michaels@GBNNews.com
To: Danica.Green@GBNNews.com
Subject: Your Assignment – Edrick Stone

Hi, Danica,

"*Mr. Gates wanted me to remind you of the importance of your assignment. Getting the insight into Edrick Stone's life and his wealth is your only objective. He said to note for you that you could easily go from an investigative journalist to a broadcast journalist after this story breaks, especially if there are secrets that can be revealed around how he's earned his wealth in stock trading. I've attached a file on what happened to his wife and son on that trip to Honduras five years ago where they died in an automobile accident. Mr. Gates thought that having this information could help you get close to Mr. Stone. Use whatever you have to in order to get the story. The exposé on him will be big. He said to remind you that you are to get the story by any means necessary. Don't forget, your career at GBN depends on it.*"

Danica Green slammed her laptop closed in

1

frustration. Sliding it from her lap to the space next to her on the bed in her hotel suite, she shook her head wondering why the reminder email from her assistant worked on her nerves. She knew what she had to do.

Looking fretfully around, her eyes landed on her luggage all nicely packed and ready for her morning flight from Seattle, Washington to Denver, Colorado. This would be her second flight in the same number of days. Her first had been from Chicago, where she lived and worked to Seattle so that she could board the plane that would bring her face to face with Edrick Stone. This was the game; he was the assignment. Stretching her neck, she tried to remove the uncomfortable feeling she felt about the plan that she hoped would benefit her. Still, there were a few reservations. If it hadn't been the Christmas holiday, she may have said no. With her current state of mind, she would do anything that would keep her mind off of the season. She'd been up all night working on how she would play her hand. She was nothing if she wasn't creative. She wasn't an actress, but she was about to play one on the flight. It had to be played this way if she was going to achieve her goal.

Danica was incensed that her assistant, Hailey, would send her an email with the words, *'by any means necessary'*. She didn't like that those words reminded her of her past. It was clear when she was hired as a journalist at *Global Blaze Network News*, the country's number one news publishing and media outlet, that everyone knew about the scandal that rocked the news world five years ago. She was already bothered that each year, her mind went to her past, but to know that others, who also knew her past, could be using her for their own ill-gotten-gain, troubled her. She wanted her mistakes to remain in the past, not brought up when someone else wanted to. That was a pretty rough time for her.

Flopping back on the bed whose comforter wasn't as soft as she had hoped it would be, she thought back to a time when she had been an equal partner in an affair that ended a man's marriage. That breaking news story had eventually ruined his network news empire along with her up and coming career as a broadcast journalist. That terrible time in her life had taken her five years to come back from with this new job. She had to get this right to not end up in another news-worthy storyline. She was a fighter; a hustler. She knew she would one day get her career back on track after a scandal that embarrassed her and her family. Now was her time to get back in the game.

By any means necessary. She shook her body from side to side trying to shake the idea of those words. They couldn't really mean that, could they? Did her boss at GBN really want her to do any and everything to get the story? Danica briefly questioned who she was now. Would she do anything to get back on top? She'd done that kind of move before it that didn't pan out well for her. Taking the assignment, she was hoping to show that she was all-in to do what it took to prove she was no longer the intern who got involved with a media mogul, thinking she as in love. She wanted to be a team player. Her last scandal landed her in a world pretty much all alone. She had been young and stupid five years ago, but not anymore. Now, she was determined to prove her worth. What she wasn't clear about was if she was ready to make her way to the top by any means necessary. Thinking about the implications of not doing her job and what that could mean, Danica opened her laptop once again, found the email and sent her reply. After all, she was a team player, as she continued to repeat to herself for a month.

"Got it."

She again slammed it shut, stood and went over to the window to look out into the snowy night. A storm was approaching, in more ways than one. It was a few days before Christmas, so seeing snow in December wasn't a surprise; that storm, she could predict and push aside without a worry. The storm that she wasn't prepared for would be the one that could tank her career once again, if she didn't get it right. She had to succeed. She had to get a better memory out of Christmas than the one that had ruined her life; made her family ashamed and thrust into the spotlight against their desire. This was her chance to make all things right again. Could she be this person? Could she work to take down a man's life and career the way hers had been taken down without a second glance or consideration from anyone? Tomorrow, she would find out.

Pulling the top of her pink and white wool two-piece pajamas set tightly across her chest, Danica walked back to the bed and climbed in. She was prepared to spend the rest of the night reading more of the back story of her own life that had been created specifically for this assignment. She was about to be a different woman with a different career all for the sake of being as anonymous as she could.

Opening the folder before her, she gazed into the face and alluring eyes of Edrick Stone. This was a man who had been celebrated as the sexiest man alive years ago. She could definitely see why. The man on photo paper was mesmerizing. If he was anything close to this good looking in person, she was in trouble. How could anyone see him and see a target for an undercover story and not imagine him under a cover in a very different way? Certainly not her. She was still a woman and he appeared to be gazing at her; through her. She shook off the thought. She couldn't repeat any past mistake which, back then, started with a handsome face and charming personality. She settled in to read less about him and more about who she needed to be. She was on assignment. She had to remember that first and foremost.

1

Danica tensed her body into a straight, barely moving stance in her seat as she gripped the airplane armrests on either side of her. Taking in a huge nerve-wracking breath, she pressed her head back against the plush leather seating of her first-class seat. If she had never been scared of flying in her life, now was that happening moment.

Closing her eyes, she silently prayed. The fact that she agreed to a secret assignment two days before Christmas, she was assuming this was karma paying her an early visit. After all, in a sense, she was up to no good. The very idea of trying to get close enough to the elusive asset manager, trading extraordinaire, investor and overall rich businessman, Edrick Stone, wasn't a good one the moment she was approached with the idea. Now, here she was on a plane, across the aisle from him and praying that the plane wouldn't take a nosedive and plunge them all to their deaths. It was a terrible thing to think about while on a plane, but flying wasn't something she enjoyed doing. She wouldn't say that openly to anyone, considering the fact that her new job as an investigative journalist will most likely send her all over the world for stories. First, she had to get through this storm and her first story focused on diving into the very private life of the drop-dead gorgeous man sitting across from her. The few glances she was able to send his way, she wondered how he was showing no signs that the storm that's rocking their plane from side to side was bothering him. Edrick was a solid, calm, non-moving passenger. He had trust in the flight crew that she was still struggling to acquire. The storm was a rough one.

Edrick's aura breathed power, strength and finesse. He was sitting with his legs crossed, hands rested on them with his eyes looking out of the small window into the heart of the storm. She remembered slamming her own shade down, not caring to see what was happening outside. She could feel it on the inside of the plane just fine. She wanted to run and jump into his arms for safety. She had a feeling a move like that would calm her even if it wasn't the best idea.

Why the man was still single five years after the death of his wife and only child, she didn't know. From what she was able to dig up on him so far, he was the perfect specimen. He wasn't just fine as the best wine, but he was a powerful businessman and presents well in everything he wears. He was a perfect contrast from the last man she'd been involved with. Being with

Ryan, a man she'd gone out on a blind date with by way of her best friend, Layla, had been a terrible idea. She hadn't dated in a while and decided to go with it. Ryan would never been seen in a suit, while Edrick's had to cost him a few thousand dollars. Ryan got nervous when he sat in the passenger seat as she drove through the Chicago streets. Edrick barely blinked as the plane bobbed and weaved. When she and Ryan were out on dates, he would barely pay attention to anything she had to say. Since being on the flight out of Seattle, Edrick seemed to willingly take in every word she said, making eye contact and responding in kind. She'd never felt a level of comfort with any man like she felt with him in the couple of hours they'd been on the flight. How could she feel so drawn to a man in such a short span of time? She knew that she was already forgetting about her reason for being on the flight; that wasn't good. Prying into his life, she just may find out. Perhaps there was a woman in his life who was as much in awe of him as she was. If so, what a lucky woman she would be. He was entitled to secrets. Of course, he had secrets. After all, if his life were an open book, she wouldn't have to pretend to be someone she isn't in order to get the story her boss, Warren Gates was expecting her to get.

The plane dipped and Danica let out a high-pitched yelp. She opened her eyes wide and without moving her head, she, again, looked to see if Edrick was showing any signs of fright. She could hear the man and woman in the seats behind her praying. Others shrieked as she had, but not Edrick. He was now flipping through a magazine like nothing was happening. She tapped her feet nervously. How was he not as terrified as she was? When his eyes caught on to hers, she couldn't look away. She was stifled by fear.

"Danica? Are you okay?" Edrick asked. The concern in his voice was loud and clear in the way he said her name. Though the melodious sound of his deep, baritone and almost husky like voice had been music to her ears throughout the flight, the caring tone eluded her, strictly out of anxiety.

With terror raging through her body as the plane tilted sharply to the left and then to the right, Danica wanted to say yes, but she was clinching her teeth together so tight that no words could find their way to her lips. She nodded her head instead and kept her eyes on him. His calmness slowly eased its way over to her.

"How are you this calm? If this plane doesn't stop all of this dipping and dodging, I'm going to lose my breakfast and my lunch," she admitted.

Edrick chuckled causing her to do the same. Danica felt like a little kid. She knew she had to be a sight from his vantage point. Slowly, she eased the grip on the armrest when the plane appeared to level out; at least for the moment.

"This is a pretty bad storm. I've been through many of them before. I thought this one wouldn't be on this path. I checked early this morning and the storm was headed in a different direction. I understand, it took an unexpected turn. Even with that, we should be fine if we can get out of the path and find a way around it. From what I can tell from news outlets I've been listening to, this one came out of nowhere. It's dumping large loads of snow everywhere."

Danica nodded. She thought about checking the news after the flight attendants did a terrible job of reassuring them that the storm wasn't that bad. Instead, she chose to listen to music. Her favorite singer, Anthony Hamilton had been serenading her with his song, *The Best of Me*, over and over as the storm began to rage. The great conversation with Edrick had temporarily ceased as it had with others on the flight. Everyone became aware of the severity of what was happening outside. When the music no longer worked, she snatched the wireless earphones from her ear and did like everyone else; she prayed.

"To think we started out so well," she said.

Danica was happy for the reprieve from worrying.

"I agree. We were doing a good job of talking while flying and then the storm hit. I take it you're not big on flying?" he asked.

"As a traveling nurse, I do some flying, but mostly, I drive everywhere."

Danica held a straight face as she continued on with the lie that was her cover story for who she was. Edrick couldn't find out her real identity. Luckily, just in case he decided to look her up, he wouldn't find much on Danica Johnson, her cover name. There wouldn't be too much yet on Danica Green either since Green was her father's last name. She had changed back to Green from King, her mother's maiden name after her life crashed and burned. When her career began, she loved how strong and powerful the last name, King, sounded. The scandal destroyed that. She was happy that even that name has since died on the lips and minds of anyone who remembered the story. Green now works. For this assignment, Johnson would need to suffice.

"You mentioned you were on your way to Spain to finally relax? I know the medical industry has been pushed to its limits the past few years. I'm sure your time off is well deserved," Edrick noted.

Danica smiled with a closed mouth, hating that she had to lie in order to connect with Edrick. It was bad enough that she allowed the farce to begin with an uncomfortable request from her leadership. They reminded her that this is the kind of thing a journalist does. This is the story that she needed for people to take her seriously. They wanted the scoop on Edrick, a man who was a mystery to so many. His anonymity was intriguing. The time for her to decline has passed. She was in character and had to keep it up, despite having a change of heart after only two hours.

"It is," she replied holding to her story as a nurse.

"You chose Christmas to take a holiday by yourself? Do you at least have friends or perhaps a family member or two in Spain?" he inquired.

Danica wanted to talk about him. He was the target, not her personal life. Still, it felt good to admit to herself that it was refreshing to meet a man who was genuinely interested in her. Her thoughts went back to Ryan who only wanted to talk about himself and never her. She thought she was a good judge of character.

Edrick was intriguing.

"I don't know what I was thinking. It was a place I'd never been too before and so, here I am," she lied.

The idea of going to Spain was a welcomed one when she found out where she was going. She only wished she were going to truly just enjoy herself.

"What part of Spain are you going to?" he asked.

"Madrid. I hear it's beautiful."

Danica talked through her carefully crafted life. It was easy to do since she'd been practicing her story for over a week. Her assistant, Hailey, did a good job of pulling together a good background story for why she was going to Spain; specifically, to the same city, Madrid, where she knew Edrick called home for most of the year, especially around Christmas. That was the time of year that his wife and son had died in Honduras while she was on a mission's trip. He was to join her and his son the day that they died in a car accident when the jeep she had been driving had gone over an embankment and killed them instantly.

"Really? I guess in all of this talking we've been doing, I never asked what part of Spain you were going to. I live in Madrid. Yes, it's a beautiful city. You will love it."

To see Edrick light up when he spoke of home had her forgetting all about the case. He had actually turned his body even more toward her, beaming with all of his pearly whites showing.

"I'm looking forward to it. I've been trying to figure out all the great places to eat and visit. My family thinks I'm crazy going over the holiday season, but I needed a break. I needed fresh ground for my time off. Not knowing anyone makes it a little harder to travel a new place without knowing the hot spots, but I do love a challenge."

"Ah, I see. It's the challenge that drove you to be on this rocky flight from Seattle to Denver and then on to Spain. Be prepared for even more snow. If you were hoping to escape bad weather, Spain this time of year, isn't the place to be," Edrick joked.

"It's okay. If I were going to stay in the States, I would be in Chicago where my parents live and that snow is no joke. Besides, I'm used to snow living in Seattle."

Danica caught herself. That wasn't a part of her background story. Her mother and step-father actually did live in Chicago not too far from her. She forgot all about using the story that her family lives in Florida. She needed to distance herself as much from her true reality as possible; especially her family. It's the eyes, she thought to herself. There was something so dark and mysterious about Edrick's eyes that made her lose herself. She could lose all train of thought just looking into his handsome face.

Before Edrick could respond the man behind her interrupted their conversation and asked Edrick a question about Spain. As they talked, she thought about how she had brought up Chicago and all the bad memories and the real reason she hated Christmas. That reason's name is Jason Halston. Thinking about him, she should have said 'was', since he's not someone she ever wanted to know anything else about again. He is now a 'was' in her life.

Jason was the man she wished she could go back and say no to when he asked her out to dinner. He was married and she knew it, but she walked into his sneaky link trap anyway. She was blinded by the promises he made to her that could catapult her career higher and much faster than she could do on her own. That was her first mistake. Her second was trusting his promises that were made between the sheets.

Jason owned one of the country's most prominent and largest newspaper publishing houses. Some would say internationally, as well, with the large audience who subscribed world-wide. She was naïve. She tried a game she'd seen in too many movies where the women used what they had to get what they wanted. That worked for her short-term. In the long-term, not so much. She fell for it all, especially his good looks. There was no way that she could also discount how handsome he was. He turned heads everywhere. He made her feel special and she melted when he looked at her. She hated thinking about what his touch did to her. She started out with a plan but fell foolishly in love.

He'd made promises to her even before their first date. She couldn't forget that. It was the beginning of the end. She was still clueless as to how she didn't know that one day that house of cards would come crashing and burning down around her. Rebuilding her life was her goal. She's struggled to get from under that terrible time. This story on Edrick was going to do that; it had to. She wanted to be a journalist since she was a little girl playing with her dolls. She would line them up like an audience and play news anchor. She chuckled to herself remembering using one of her Barbie Dolls as a microphone. She thought she had finally gotten the chance to live out her dream. Nothing prepared her for how wrong she was. Having the extra time to think about things on this flight while talking with the most delightful man, something about her plan no longer sat well with her.

It wasn't until she started doing her research on his past that Danica realized taking on the job was a bad idea. In the time being on the plane, she found Edrick damn-near irresistible. What was it with her and men? It had to be something considering the dating slump her life was currently in the midst of.

"Sorry about that," Edrick said breaking into her thoughts.

It appears his conversation was done and he was back to her. She actually like him. The way he smiled and gazed at her, she liked him. He was more than words on paper.

"That's okay. We're going to Spain and you're an expert," she admitted.

"You mentioned Chicago. I love Chicago. It's one of my favorite places to visit when I come to the U.S. I spend a lot of time there and in New York."

"So, you live in Spain full-time? That's amazing. I pegged you for a U.S. citizen," she said.

Danica was digging, but not too much. She didn't want to scare him off. She had to do something to keep from staring at him with the desire to lick across her lips with the remembrance of how sexy and powerfully manly he looked walking through the airport to get on the flight.

"I used to live here in New York. I still keep my apartment there, but I consider Spain home. I moved about four years ago."

Danica waited to see if he would share more, but he didn't. A somber look came over his face. When he looked away from her and down at his phone, she knew his last words had brought back a memory he didn't want to have at this moment. She knew how he felt. There were things she didn't want to think about, but being on this flight brought it all back.

"Well, Spain must have been a good place to move to since you're still calling it home."

Just then, the plane dipped again. She was happy that they were only thirty minutes from the Denver airport. They were in for a three-hour layover before getting back in the air for their then non-stop flight to Spain. Between now and then, she had to make enough of a connection that she would get to see him while she was there. She needed to think of a plan. She was good at flirting. It was clear they each has some level of interest in each other. They were going to be in Madrid together.

"Don't be afraid. We're almost to Denver. Phillip is the best pilot you could be flying with. I've flown with him many, many times and he's the best," Edrick asserted.

"I guess that's why you can be so calm."

"That's exactly why."

Danica was about to say something else when Edrick's phone rang. He pointed to it letting her know he had to take the call. She smiled and laid her head back. No longer holding onto the armrest with a death-grip, Danica leaned back and attempted to enjoy the flight. Unfortunately, all she could think about was her reason for hating the Christmas holiday season. Most of all, her hatred for flying. She tried to think of something else, but that dreadful Christmas day flight from Chicago to Paris played back in her head as if she were watching it as a spectator. The plane calmed and so did she. She could hear Edrick talking business. She should be listening to see what else she could garner from him, but her mind was playing tricks on her. She was going on a trip down memory lane even if she didn't want to.

"This trip is going to be the best time of your life," Jason exclaimed proudly.

Danica smiled as they held hands while sitting close together on Jason's private jet. She never expected that this would be her life, or sort of her life. She was actually living a part of her life on the downlow, but she had also never been this happy. She was all shades of wrong sitting and holding hands with a married man, but she'd fallen hard for him. He came at her hard with his smoothness and charisma. She felt no shame about falling for it all.

"We're spending Christmas out of the country. I can't tell you how I have longed to go to the Maldives. Then we're headed to Paris for a few days. It's the perfect romantic getaway," Danica said excitedly bouncing around in her chair. She could hardly contain herself. Maldives was all pleasure. Their trip to Paris would have some fun included, but mostly, Jason had some business to take care of. She was just happy that he made sure she was a part of it all.

"Let me get you some wine, baby."

Danica watched Jason signal for the flight attendant. In the next instant, there was an expensive bottle of Chateau Lafite Rothschild 2018, a French wine that Jason knew was her favorite.

"A girl could continue to get used to being spoiled by you," she swooned against his arm.

Jason picked up the two glasses now filled with wine and handed one to her. Taking a sip, she took a moment to allow the taste to soothe her entire body.

"You have really worked your magic on me this past year. I know it's still a little weird and all, but you make me happy," Jason admitted.

He kissed her on the lips before taking his own sip.

"I'm happy, Jason."

Danica started to say more, but let the words live in her head. As happy as she was, the situation wasn't one that led to a happy future for them together and that bothered her. The more time they spent sneaking around to spend time together, the harder she fell for him.

Turning from him, she held her glass and looked out of the window as the plane took off from Chicago O'Hare airport on their way to the time of their lives. She was headed to a romantic Christmas and New Year's Eve with a man who worships her. Yet, her mind was on the families left behind whose heads were filled with lies. She had never lied to her family until she met Jason. She hated missing time with her family. This was the year she was going to spend the holiday with her father, step-mother, her younger brother and his girlfriend, someone he had just started dating. She had an older step-brother, her step-mother's son from a previous marriage, who was also going to join them with his wife and kids. They had been looking forward to her joining them in Miami for the holiday. She told them that she was working on her first feature story. She explained that the story was taking her on location, one that she couldn't disclose, but that they would be very happy for her when the story broke. There was no story; at least not for her. Jason promised her that he would take a high-profile story from another reporter at the newspaper and give it to her. He owned the newspaper publishing house, which meant he could do whatever he wanted to do.

"Are you? I'm looking at your face and you went from smiling to sullen in a matter of seconds. I made this trip happen and you know what I had to sacrifice to do it. You should be smiling for eleven straight days," he said.

Exhaling, she turned back to him. Their loving moment was about to be laced with ire.

"I've never lied to my family the way I have throughout this year. I know what you sacrificed. I didn't approach you, you approached me."

"True, but it's Christmas and I gave up this time to be with you and not at home with my kids."

"And Mariah?" she asked.

The mention of Jason's wife got a rise out of him. His quirky smile disappeared.

"Don't go there. I'm not the only person in this affair. You jumped into this and continue to do so with both feet," he snorted. Danica didn't want this. She didn't want their trip to be laced with anger. She still needed to know what her future looked like.

"You think I don't know what I've been doing? Yes, it's fun, but what woman really wants to do all of this sneaking around?" she demanded.

"Wait, a minute ago you were happy. Now, you have a problem sneaking around? I was married when you met me. Every single time you slip in between the sheets with me, I'm still married. I have much more to lose than you do. If you have another way to do this, let me know."

"So, in other words, this is a win-win for you. And me?" she asked.

"What do you want? If this is another talk about my wife, you know that situation. I don't have a pre-nuptial agreement. If we split, she gets half of everything I own. I told you, I'm planning on us being together. In three years, my last kid will graduate from high school. They'll all be grown. I just need a little more time, I told you that."

"In the meantime, I'm seeing someone I can't tell anyone about. I can't be seen with you in public. We make loving eyes around the office, but can't show any display of affection. How long before someone finds out?" she asked.

Danica had seen the stares and heard the whispers. She was edgy all the time that someone would find out that she was sleeping with the boss. She would never be trusted in her field again or in any field.

Before Jason could respond, both of his cellphones began pinging like crazy. She had turned hers off once they boarded the plane. He reached for it, checking the message. She was about to continue on when the look on Jason's face made her think that someone had died. He started scrolling through his phone so fast, she feared what may have happened.

"Oh, my god, no."

He spoke so low that Danica barely heard him.

"What's wrong? Is someone hurt?" she asked, trying to look over his shoulder to see what he was reading.

"No!" Jason then shouted. Danica jumped and panicked.

"You're scaring me," she shouted. "What?" she yelled in horror.

"It's over; it's all over. I'm done. My life, it's over. Everything I've worked for. It's all over. Because of you, it's all over."

The words Jason spoke shocked her. Combining them with the look of disgust on his face, she was suddenly frightened.

"What?"

Danica's voice cracked. She felt herself on the verge of tears. She was scared. She reached for Jason. To her dismay, he stood and moved away from her as he continued to frantically looked through, not just one, but both of his phones. He then rushed to his duffle on another seat and pulled out his iPad. She saw his breathing increase as if he had just run a marathon. She could see his fingers literally shaking as he keyed in letters or numbers, but whatever was going on, was getting worse. Out of his mouth flew one expletive after another.

"What did you do?" Jason asked harshly.

"What? What did I do? About what? I didn't do anything," she stammered.

"Danica – what the hell did you do?"

Before she could reply, Jason turned his iPad around and showed her. His hand was shaking so bad that she had a hard time focusing on what he was showing her. And then, she saw it. She needed the world to swallow her whole.

"Oh, my god. Where did you get that?" she asked as he scrolled through one picture of them after another, with several of the pictures of them in compromising positions. She had taken them. She had taken all of the pictures. How did he get them?

"I'm asking you again – what did you do? Who did you send these to? They are all over every newspaper, television station and gossip rag. Where is your phone? You had to have taken these?" he chastised.

Before he continued and before she could answer him, she grabbed her phone and with nervous fingers, she punched in her code. She saw him reading something new on his phone at the same time.

"I didn't take all of those. We're in a lot of them together."

"Yeah – well, listen to this. It's a text from Mariah."

'Just when you decided to take your sneaky-link on your little getaway instead of being at home with your wife and children, I've shared your love affair with the world. I will expect my half in the divorce, but in the meantime, tell her to never trust leaving her phone around the office for anyone to get a hold of. Your employees are just as loyal to me as they used to be to you. Have fun in the Maldives you slithering snake!'

"Ladies and gentlemen, we are about to land in Denver."

The announcement snapped Danica out of reminiscing about the past. Jason had quickly cancelled their plans and headed back to Chicago to fix his marriage. He never said another word to her on the flight or once they landed. She learned from human resources that she was fired and would receive a huge severance package. Her life was over; until now.

2

Edrick wasn't a person who worried much these days. Sitting in Denver National Airport waiting for the three-hour layover to end, he checked his watch several times. He wasn't even sure why. Usually with a layover in Denver, he would have contacted one of his best friends in the world, Albert London, who owned several exclusive winter resorts in Denver. Albert and his wife would make the trip to the airport to see him even if it was just for a few minutes over a cup of coffee. He wanted to contact them this time, but knew that they would be busy with Christmas coming up in two days. Besides that, the storm that was now circling Denver would put them in danger if they tried to venture out; he knew they would try. It's been a long time since they've seen him in person. Though they understood why, it was still a conversation that never turned out well. He wasn't ignoring them, as they would like to claim. He still had a lot to deal with when it came to the memories of his family being at the resort. Without them, the struggle was real.

There had been a time when he couldn't wait to get to the resort. Times have changed over five years. Any of their four resorts saw tons of visitors every Christmas. This time of year used to be a good time for him too; not so much anymore. He tossed around the idea of calling them and not calling them since the plane landed. He didn't want to take them away from their busy season. He knew that even with that, he would have made that call from the airplane. There were a few things that distracted him today. There was the storm. There was the holiday that he wanted to spend alone in Spain; away from the resort. Finally, there was the very beautiful woman who sat in the seat across from him in first class. Her name was Danica Johnson.

For two hours he talked to her. Now, he just wanted the chance to learn more. This feeling was different for him. He hadn't been a monk since his wife died, but he left feelings for any woman at the door. He left any desire to spend more than one night with any woman. He fought being in any kind of personal relationship or working toward one. Women were a means to mutual gratification which he made clear up front. That was the important choice he'd made. Something about Danica had him thinking about more.

The minute he saw her at the airport in Seattle, he Hadn't been able to take his eyes off of her. That's saying a lot when it comes to him. He'd spent the past five years of his live focused on nothing but work. He had the occasional date, but no woman had garnered this much attention from him since...

Edrick didn't complete the thought. He already knew the name and the face of the only woman he'd ever fallen head over heels in love with. This attraction he was feeling toward Danica was, in logically thinking, new for him. He'd sworn off the idea of getting close to a woman other than to satisfy his carnal needs. This time of year, was especially hard. Christmas wasn't a season he looked forward to. There was something about Danica, besides her beauty, that drew him to her immediately. He didn't want the feeling, but he was enjoying the view.

A few times, he'd caught her checking him out too. That wasn't unusual for him to garner that kind of attention. What was rare was how he didn't care that she'd caught him gazing at her. He couldn't help himself. She was gorgeous.

From what he could tell, Danica was about five-eight, though he couldn't be too positive. In the airport in Seattle, she had been bundled up like a snow bunny to protect herself from the cold. Once on the plane, she removed her thick purple winter coat and underneath was a shape he couldn't stop gazing at. She was all natural born and curves that had no end; the kind he loved on a woman. Everything about her roared at him. Inwardly, he growled back in response, like a lion ready to bring her into the fold. Wanting her was obvious, if to no one else, then definitely to himself. Being seated right across from him, he couldn't have been luckier. They connected instantly, not just with words, but there was something in the air between them that grabbed a whole of every part of his being and wouldn't turn him loose. The way her lips curved into a sexy smile to the left side stirred his body to life. He loved lips on a woman. Danica's were perfect. No woman had ever had that kind of an impact on him since...

There he was again. Edrick couldn't stop going to the past and remembering the last time his heart and spirit recognized a woman.

As if he had willed her to appear, Danica showed up in the airport waiting area holding tight to a hot cup of coffee. Before walking away, she'd asked him if she could bring him a cup but he declined. He was too focused on when they would be able to board. The weather in Denver was getting pretty brutal by the minute, something they could all see through the large paned glass at the airport. A nagging feeling was telling him that his plan of spending a quiet Christmas in Spain was about to be derailed.

"Still no word?" she asked him when she took the seat across from him in the area where all of the passengers who were on the plane with them waited. It was now four hours after they landed for a layover that should have been over already. They were all waiting on a word of what was next.

"Nothing at all. I just checked the weather and it's looking pretty bad. This storm that we came through turned and followed us here. They are calling for two feet of snow, and in some places ice, to drop in this area before the sun rises in the morning."

Just then the announcement came that the flight out of Denver to Spain was cancelled. People around them began shouting and complaining about what they were going to do. Christmas was coming up and they all had plans for the holiday. Edrick was lucky. He didn't have any real plans other than to spend time at his home sulking about the emptiness he felt every year around this time. He had money, prestige and power, but none of that compared to the hole in his heart that nothing seemed to fill. The spark in his very being appear to be dimmed forever.

"What are we going to do? Are there any hotels around here?" Danica asked him. He was surprised at how calm she was considering the rack of nerves she was on the plane. Perhaps, like everyone else but him, she was shocked into the reality that they weren't going anywhere; they were officially stuck in Denver. He could deal. It was clear that the people around him were lost.

Edrick looked at Danica and then to the many families gathered around talking to one other with despair. He counted about three dozen, maybe a few people more, in total. He didn't get to answer her when, Phillip, the pilot from the flight and a close friend of his, walked over as everyone gathered around him.

"I'm sorry folks, but we are grounded. I know you heard the announcement, but I wanted to also come over and tell you myself. The storm that is upon us here is about to get even worse. I know this is bad news and I'm sorry. It's safer to extend the layover to late tomorrow or maybe even Christmas morning. It can't be helped. I know you have plans, but for now, we will do our best to help you find accommodations for tonight. I know that's not a consolation, but it's the best we can do. You don't want to be here at the airport when the storm hits and you can't get out. I've seen people try and sleep on the chairs and floors around here and It's not a solace for having to be here."

"Where will we go?" someone asked.

Edrick looked at Danica and wondered what she would do. He hated that they were all stranded, especially the kids.

"Will Santa find us?" a little girl asked.

"How long will we be here?" yet another passenger asked.

"I don't have money for a hotel room. I spent it all on this trip. Will the airline foot that bill?" an older gentleman asked.

"Everyone, I know you have a lot of questions. I don't have all the answers right now, but there are employees who are working on a plan for each of you. Again, I'm sorry. We're working fast because the storm will soon close the airport. I'm going to see how much progress has been made and I'll be right back," Phillip said.

Before he walked away, Edrick stopped him and pulled him to the side.

"Phil, how long are we stranded for? Truth," he added.

"A full day, maybe two."

"Christmas day?" Edrick inquired.

"Most likely, yes. This storm is massive. It wasn't predicted but it's here. We're doing all we can."

Edrick moved him even further away from the mass of people who were now gathered around two airline employees who walked over to try and calm the rowdy crowd.

"I may be able to help. Let me make a phone call and see what I can do. I'm going to call Al. You know him. I happen to be best friends with the one person I know who may be able to help with accommodations; at least I hope so."

"Edrick, you are the best. I also want to thank you for convincing my daughters to take your investment advice. They didn't believe me when I told them what you've done for the wife and I through the years," Phillip celebrated.

"I'm glad I was able to help. Being social influencers, your girls have acquired quite a large income from promoting on their platforms. Investing early is the best idea for the bulk of that income. It will keep them from wasting a lot of that money."

"They're stocks are doing well, even in this economy. Looks like I'll be stuck here too, missing them."

Edrick nodded. He knew how much his friend loved his family. The flight to Spain was to be Phillip's last until after the new year. He felt for him. At one time, he had his own family to rush home to.

"Well, I'm going to, hopefully, work out something nice for us all. Give me a minute," Edrick explained while reaching for his phone. Looks like he was going to be seeing Albert and Misha after all.

"Great. I'll try and calm the crowd. The kids seem the most lethal!" Phillip explained.

"Dude, you're talking about Santa. They are lethal when it comes to Santa not finding them," he laughed while punching in the number to Albert's cell.

As he waited for him to pick up, Edrick looked toward Danica. For the first time, he wasn't in a rush to spend Christmas in Spain. He may get his chance to get to know her better. It was planned, but here he was; possibly getting a chance to have a reason to enjoy Christmas again.

"Ed! Is that you?" Albert shouted in the phone.

Edrick chuckled. Albert was the only person allowed to call him, Ed.

"Bro, of course it's me!"

"Well, I can't say I was expecting a call from you, but I will say I'm glad you're calling. Misha told me she called you about coming here for Christmas this year.

When we didn't hear back from you, I told her to let it go. How are you? I'm always thinking about you this time of year. I hope that one year, you'll take us up on the invitation to spend Christmas around people."

"You just may get your wish this year. I'm here in Denver at the airport."

"What? You didn't tell us you were coming in."

"That wasn't the plan. You know how I am about Christmas."

"Yeah, I know. That's why I wouldn't let Misha pester you this year. We miss her and the baby too. Misha talks about our good times together all the time. What brings you to Denver in the middle of this ginormous storm that's about to bring a few feet of snow. Of course, as the owner of four ski resorts and several Chalets and cabins, romantic and family focused, it's an extra Christmas gift for us."

"Are you fully booked?" Edrick asked.

"No. We actually have quite a few rooms and suites available at the new resort. We weren't expecting to have it ready by Christmas. Due to your expertise with investing and asset management, the builders were excited to get that influx of cash if they were able to stick to the schedule. We weren't sure they would make it, so we didn't include that in the booking packages. We have a few people who have switched over. Those were our frequent guests who visit throughout the year. What's up? You need a room? Are we actually going to have you here for Christmas?" Albert asked.

Edrick couldn't believe it himself, but it looks like he was going to spend Christmas someplace other than Spain. Was he ready? Turning again, he saw Danica out of the corner of his eye and he knew it was time. Maybe this Christmas, he wouldn't have to hate the holiday as much as he'd come to.

"Actually, I need several rooms. I had a layover for a few hours and with the storm, that layover is being extended not just for me, but for everyone on the flight I was on. We have about forty or fifty people, most are families. Think you can accommodate? Before you jump right in with your hospitality, I'm going to cover the cost. Don't try and change my mind or we'll be on the phone forever. I can't see these families stranded here at the airport or at some hotel with nothing to do for Christmas. Because I know your lovely wife, I already know she goes all out for the holidays. I suspect there is a Santa in the midst? We have families with kids who are upset thinking Santa won't find them," he explained.

"Imagine you caring about Santa. Do you remember the many times you played Santa Claus for us? Those were some good times. Are you kidding me? We get you for the holiday and we get to help out families? You are right up my wife's alley with this. Of course, we can accommodate everyone. Do you want your usual suite? You know Misha leaves it open every Year in honor of Phaedra and Christian. She hopes that one year you will join us. I can't wait to tell her you're here now. She will definitely have a Merry Christmas, especially if you're here on the actual day."

"I don't think I'm ready to stay in my old suite. Where are you putting everyone up at?"

"We have several Chalets available along with our signature cabins right on the resort grounds. The families may like those. In the new hotel will probably be the most feasible place to put them up, but let them decide when they get here. Each resort has their own Santa and elves with lots of activities planned. Misha goes all out and we are never short when it comes to employees. They get double pay for the holiday, so everyone wants to work. In fact, like most holidays, we have double the number of staff that we would usually have throughout the rest of the year."

"I'll stay at the hotel where you're putting everyone else."

"Great. I'll reserve the top floor suite for you. I'll get transportation out there to pick you all up. We need to move on this quickly. That storm is coming in with a force. The roads will soon be impassable."

"Albert, you are a life saver. I'll text you in a few minutes with the exact number from our flight. It may be one or two days at the most. I don't know – you may have accommodations that may make them want to stay even longer. If so, just charge everything to my account. Heather will get that payment over to you quickly."

Edrick made a mental note to email his executive assistant to make sure all costs were paid expeditiously. He'd given his team at all of his office locations the holiday off. Heather would get the message when she was back in the office after the new year came in.

"You know you don't have to, but I won't start an argument. I never win them against you."

"You're learning," Edrick acknowledged and laughed out loud.

"In a good mood and laughing like you've just hit the lottery? What else is going on? What has you this happy? I get that you're trying to help out those who are stranded, but there is a tone in your voice that I haven't heard in a long time. Something else has you smiling like a Cheshire cat, even if I can't see it. I'm hearing a little bit of the old Ed in your voice."

"There's nothing there. Stop trying to make something up. I'm always a happy, happy guy; just a happy, happy guy," Edrick sang.

"Oh, now I know something is up. Did you just sing a tune from a TikTok?"

"You're reaching, Al!"

"Who is she?" Albert asked.

Edrick didn't respond. Danica immediately came to mind when Albert made him think of a person. He'd just met her. She wasn't a woman that he would say has him making a change of heart or to have him singing funny TikTok tunes. She did have a way of making him smile. Like right now, the way she was gazing over at him, he couldn't help but delight in how his heart skipped a beat at how her smile didn't just stop at her lips, but encompassed her entire body. His desire to know more about her was definitely driving him to have a Merry Christmas for the first time in a long time. He loved how easily they dove into conversing. It has been a long time since he's look at a woman and thought beyond saying hello. Still, Albert didn't need to know any of that.

"There is no she."

"Liar. I can hear you smiling through the phone."

"It's your imagination," Edrick said, trying to derail the conversation to something else.

"Let me get off of here and get things moving. I want to be sure we have people in place to handle everyone's needs when they get here. I can't wait to connect with you, my friend. It's been too long. We worry about you always on the go and never settling down anywhere for any real length of time. You moved to Spain and we don't get to see you as much as we would like."

"We'll make up for it while I'm here. I'm looking forward to seeing my godson. I'm mad I don't have a gift for him."

Edrick hadn't seen Albert's son, Colin, in over a year in person. They video chat a lot, but that wasn't enough. He didn't want Colin growing up feeling like his godfather can't connect to him because he reminds him of his own son he lost.

"You know Misha went overboard as she tends to do on gifts and toys for Colin. Take a couple of the gifts she bought and give them to him. He won't know the difference. At six years old, he'll focus on the cheap little army men she bought him and not the real expensive stuff like what you would usually send him," Albert laughed.

"Of course, I sent him some expensive stuff this year. With this weather, I'm not sure they will get to the resort by Christmas."

"That's fine. There is a lot to go around."

Edrick smiled. He missed his best friend. When he was married, the four of them spent many vacations together. Diving into his own little world and shutting out everyone else after Phaedra and Christian's death, it wasn't until the moment he heard Albert's voice on the phone that he knew it was time to get back to life. Maybe even something new, he thought as his eyes locked with Danica's. He kept doing that. He wondered if she noticed the extra attention he kept giving her; he hoped so.

"We'll be here waiting. See you shortly," he said to Albert.

Before the line disconnected, he could hear his friend shouting for his wife, no doubt to ramp up her excitement for the holiday knowing he would be back in the fold with them.

Walking back over to the crowd, he patted Phillip on the back with a level of excitement that got his blood flowing. He was suddenly in the Christmas spirit.

"Hi, everyone. My name is Edrick Stone."

"I told you!" a man shouted.

"Thomas, be quiet. Yes, you told me that's who you thought was seated in first class. Now we all know. Be quiet," a woman said, quieting Thomas as the crowd giggled at their interaction.

"Yes, it's me. I know this situation was unexpected. I, too, was looking forward to being in Spain. As our pilot said, we are grounded. We were expecting a few hours layover and it's turning into a possible Christmas in Denver."

When a round of disappointment-laced exhales surrounded him, Edrick smiled, hoping his news would put a smile on their faces too.

"What about Santa? I wrote him and told him I would be in Spain?" a little girl looked up at him with the frown that was melting his heart. He remembered when Christian would get his way with a frown just like hers.

Edrick stooped down to talk directly to her.

"I have an idea that I think may work. See, Santa knows about the snow storm. Remember, he sees everything. I have a friend who owns several really nice places to stay here in Denver. He has offered to put everyone up in a hotel or a family cabin for tonight, tomorrow and for the whole Christmas week if anyone wants to stay longer. The best part is there are a lot of holiday activities that will be happening that you will love. There are rides, swimming indoors, skiing, roller skating, video games and best of all, Santa will be right here. He knows about all the families that are getting stranded. I hear that he will make a special trip here just to make sure you get some toys for Christmas. Now, it may not be everything you asked him for, but I know he's got the good stuff. You will still have a very, merry Christmas."

When the little girl smiled and he saw teeth missing in the front, her excitement transferred to him. He was excited that he could bring a smile to her face. He felt himself getting emotional. Not knowing who or what to thank, he knew that he needed to be at this place at this time doing exactly what he was doing. It all started with a conversation with a woman on a plane while he was headed home to avoid Christmas. The holiday was no being thrust in his face. He happily accepted it.

"Yeah!" the kids all shouted together and bounced around.

Edrick knew his job was complete as far as the kids were concerned. He now needed to deal with the adults.

"As I was saying, my friend is putting everyone up. Accepting that invitation is totally up to you. You can stay one night, two nights or the entire week. The airline will still work out a plan to either get you to

Spain, if you choose or you can stay until the new year comes in. You can make the best of this situation or you can also go with the accommodations the airline will make for you. My friend, Albert, is sending transportation to pick up everyone who wants to give the resort a try at no cost to you. I will say this – I have spent many Christmases here at the various resorts. I can attest to the fact that there are lots of things to do here that you won't be able to take them all in while you're here. There are games, casinos, movie theaters, indoor golf, nightclubs with the best live entertainment and a lot more. Most of all, you'll taste some of the best food which is all included in your stay. If you're interested, raise your hand."

Edrick barely got out the last word when every hand went up, including the captain and the flight attendants from their flight. When he turned and saw Danica's hand raised, a level of excitement that he hadn't experienced in a long time shot through him. Perhaps fate was playing a hand in his meeting her on the flight. He was praying for a chance to spend some time with her if she was interested. He couldn't wait to find out.

"Edrick, buddy, I appreciate this," Phillip said. "Okay, everyone. Follow the airline helpers here who will work to get everyone's luggage. If we have to be someplace until the storm passes, there is no better place than at a resort that specializes in a great

Christmas experience. Most of all, like Edrick said, good food!" Phillip added.

Edrick laughed harder when Phil pumped his fist in the air.

As they all walked, Edrick fell in line with Danica's steps.

"I'm glad you're staying. Perhaps you would consider joining me for dinner tonight or tomorrow? I enjoyed our talk on the plane. I'm hoping we can continue that. That is, if you're up for that."

When he was about to say more, perhaps pleading a little more, she spoke up before he could get another word out.

"I would like that. Either day would be great. How long are you planning to stay?" she asked.

"I haven't been here for Christmas in a lot of years. I miss my friends. I'm thinking of extending my layover until the new year. What about you? I know you probably have plans in Spain. I can guarantee you that if you stay, I will show you all the resort has to offer. This place is a lot of fun. You will enjoy it as much as you would if you were in Madrid. Trust me – I know. I live there. The resort is so much better. Besides, it's Christmas."

"I trust you and your opinion. I think I would like to stay the entire week also. A vacation is a vacation. It's about good company and of course, good food. You said this place has the best?" Danica asked.

"I guarantee it," he replied.

"Then I'm all yours."

The words were music to his ears. Usually, when a woman wanted more from him, he main things clear to alleviate any miscommunication about his intentions. With Danica, his intentions were all about her. The idea surprised him, but he was more than ready for it. She said she was all his. He wanted that. Quietly to himself he said, he wanted her.

3

Danica looked around her room at one of the hotels which made up the *Donegral Hotel, Residences and Resorts by London Aria*. She had no idea that Edrick coming through for them would bring about such luxury when it came to hotel stays. She was in a two-bedroom suite that had top of the line furniture which sparkled with a newness that alluded to it being as expensive as they come.

Rushing straight to one of the two master bedrooms, she found a beautifully hand stitched blue and white down comforter and Egyptian cotton sheets which had a note on them that let the guest know that the bedding was hypo-allergenic. She felt around on the bed and cheered when her hands encountered a pillow-top mattress; just like the one she had at home. They were her favorite. There was a big-screen television on the wall and enough dresser and closet space that was more than she had at home and could certainly accommodate what she had with her and then some. She was told that the resort was for short and long-term stays. She could imagine herself doing both in a place as inviting as this. Everything was exquisite.

Walking into the bathroom, there was a gorgeous gold and marble clawfoot tub with enough space for two people; she wished. She'll have to add that to one of her Christmas lists one year. Smiling to herself, she ran her hand across the towels and marveled at how plush they were. There were several plush bathrobes with a note saying she should feel free to use a new one each day. Housekeeping would replenish anything she needed as often as she needed with a quick phone call.

Venturing back out into the main area, there was another big screen television, a microwave with a full-size refrigerator, not one of the ones most hotels had that one could barely fit leftovers in. Working as a journalist, she has seen her share of hotels with good and bad accommodations. This place was amazing with everything all fresh and new. Edrick mentioned to her, while on the ride from the airport to the resort, that they would be staying in the newest resort which had just been completed two months ago, ahead of schedule. That was the reason why there was room for everyone from the flight. So many coincidences were happening in the past few hours. Was this all a part of the Christmas spirit that she had taken for granted the past few years?

There was also twenty-four-hour front desk service along with around the clock concierge services, daily housekeeping, dry cleaning service as well as laundry facilities where you could do your own laundry or someone on staff would do the laundry for you. The best feature, since she was a true foodie, was the around the clock kitchen service. She could order breakfast, lunch or dinner at any time of the day. She was definitely a breakfast at dinner kind of person. All meals were prepared specifically per the room request based on the menu available for the day.

She danced around on the beautiful dark gray hardwood floors throughout. Best of all, her suite had a small office that she could work from. That space included a printer and free wi-fi service. There was even the availability for guests to secure a hotel provided laptop if need be. With her accommodation, that service was free as well. Edrick had certainly come through. She would find a card and hand write her thank you.

The furniture in the living room wasn't your usual hotel stay loveseat that folded out into a bed. No, this was a large gray sectional that looked as comfortable as it did expensive. There was something extra special about her suite that usually would have had her cringing with disappointment. Her eyes landed on a wealth of Christmas decorations everywhere. That included a fully decorated artificial green spruce Christmas tree with accessories in shades of red and white. There were lights across the balcony outside of the bedroom and the living room areas. There were other decorations throughout including a stocking hung on the electric fireplace that sat under the television. She gasped when she noticed that her name was already added to the white area of the Christmas stocking. She wondered how they were able to do that so fast. There were other Christmas touches about and where the idea of Christmas would usually make her sad, she felt all warm and happy inside. This is the feeling that Christmas used to generate for her. One flight and one handsome man later, who came through and saved the day, and she was in the Christmas spirit. Everything about Edrick was magical.

The layover for more than a few hours was unexpected, but very welcomed. The location was different, but her assignment was still the same; she needed to get close to Edrick. Thankfully, he was making that easy by asking her to have dinner with him. She was already anticipating his company. When she spoke with him, she had to concentrate on her back story to stay on task when what she really wanted to do was be Danica Green, a woman who hadn't liked this time of year in five years, but thanks to his kind face, and personable personality, her dislike for this time of year was fading quickly. She was slowly forgetting about Danica King and little by little, Danica Johnson was also starting to fade.

When she was checking in, the associate who got her all situated told her about all of the fun things the resort had to offer, even more than Edrick had shared with her. The moment she heard about the spa, which was also open around the clock, she couldn't wait to sign up for a massage and other treatments for Christmas Eve. She was already looking forward to the holiday experience. Since she was planning to stay as long as Edrick was staying, she may as well take advantage of what the resort had to offer. The resort boasted several entertainment venues. She was excited to know that one of her favorite R&B artists would be performing the next night for a big Christmas Eve concert. Though she wasn't big on skiing, she was hoping to even give that a try.

Dancing around the suite and singing to herself, Danica realized how easy it was to forget about her assignment; the reason she was in Denver. Her company was under the assumption that she was on her way to Spain. She needed to call Hailey to have her relay the information about the change.

Searching for her phone, she dialed Hailey's cell, knowing that she would always be on the other end to respond to anything she needed.

"Hailey! I'm glad I caught you," she said the moment the line connected.

Danica took a seat in the middle of the sectional and delighted in the feeling of floating on a soft cloud, yet firm for comfort.

"Danica, I was hoping to hear from you. I saw on the news that a terrible storm was covering all of Denver. Were you able to get your flight out before it hit?"

"No, I'm still in Denver."

"That's a bummer. Mr. Gates won't be happy about that. What about Edrick Stone? Did you make any real contact with him? Is he still there too?"

Danica looked at the phone and sucked her teeth. It was all about the story on Edrick that mattered.

"Yes, I did and yes, he is here in Denver snowed in, too. Everyone on the flight was. He has a friend who owns the largest resorts here and was able to get this friend to put us all up until flights out resumed after the storm. I was calling to tell you about that. I may be staying here longer instead of going to Spain."

Danica was about to explain why when Hailey cut her off.

"That's not good news. You're supposed to follow Edrick to Madrid and get him to be comfortable enough with you that he would share about himself. Perhaps, invite you to his house and you could do some snooping."

Danica exhaled with frustration. Hailey was a great assistant, but she didn't listen well. She always assumed the worse in everything.

"Hailey, you didn't let me finish."

"Oh, sorry. Go ahead. I'm taking notes."

"Edrick decided that he wanted to stay and visit with his friends through the holiday instead of traveling to Spain. He asked me if I was interested in enjoying the holiday here and I said yes."

"Oh stop! He likes you already? Just that fast? You work quick."

Once again, Danica exhaled loudly in frustration. If she didn't know any better, she would take Hailey's comment as an insult. Was she a toad or something? Was she not attractive and appealing? Why did it sound like a surprise to Hailey that in a few hours, Edrick found something in her he liked? She certainly found everything about him likeable. He was exactly what a hot-blooded woman would love for Santa to plant under her tree.

Sitting up straight, she found herself losing focus again. Edrick was a job and she needed to remember that. He'd already moved her mind from hating Christmas to loving everything about it with the help of the beautiful decorated resort.

"Hailey, I didn't say all of that. He invited everyone from the plane to stay the entire week. He's footing the bill. When all of this is over, he'll need to be reimbursed. I don't think he will take kindly to what I'm doing."

"He's even paying for you to stay? My, what did you do to get him in the palm of your hand already?"

"Nothing. Stop making this about just me. He felt bad that holiday plans were derailed for everyone on the flight. He's kindhearted like that, I guess. He's actually quite a nice guy. He doesn't seem like the type that would be out here swindling people out of their money with a Ponzi scheme. I don't see it," Danica explained.

Without thinking, she started nibbling on her purple and white manicured nails as she wondered why she was all of a sudden in the Edrick Stone cheering section.

"Be careful, Danica. You're not supposed to fall for the guy. Everyone has secrets; you should know that first-hand. Have you learned anything that you want me to report back on yet? I'll let everyone know that you're in Denver, but so is the target. Anything else?" Hailey asked.

Danica opened her mouth to speak and then shut it just as fast. Target? Hailey had called Edrick 'the target'. Now that she heard someone else say it, when she said it to herself, she didn't realize how horrible it sounded referring to him that way. What an awful way to refer to anyone. In a matter of hours, she was already second-guessing what her boss thought that she would find. This kind, sexy, gorgeous of a specimen that Edrick was wouldn't hurt or scam anyone. She still couldn't let go of the story of how his wife and five-year old son had died. It was tragic. She didn't know if she could persevere the way he has.

"Nothing for now. I'll email you any updates."

"Good. Try to get him talking about business and anything that I can check into. This story, if it leads to a scandal, will be huge for the network. You could be in the anchor seat in no time. Personally, I think it's time they replaced Marilyn in that broadcast anchor seat. With your youth and beauty, you would bring in a new, younger audience. She's what, going on fifty? She's ancient."

When Hailey broke out into a loud laugh, Danica didn't join her. The comment was crude, out of order and unnecessary. She knew what breaking out a story on Edrick could do for her carrier, but trying to replace Marilyn, a woman she respected and who offered to help her get into a broadcast journalist role was not ancient. She was highly regarded and respected. Danica felt like the woman truly wanted to help her get her career back on track. She decided to ignore the comment.

"Are you working tomorrow? I know it will be Christmas Eve, but if I have something and I email it to you, will you be on the other end?" Danica asked. She wanted to get the conversation back to where it needed to be. She didn't like it but it was better than where their chat was headed, defaming another woman in broadcasting.

"I'm working throughout the holiday, just like you; even on Christmas day. Mr. Gates is hoping to have something big to kickstart the new year. A story on Edrick, especially if it's juicy and laced with scandal, would be just what we need. Just remember that if this turns out well, it would mean big promotions and bonuses for the whole team. I know I could use a bonus and a promotion out of being an assistant. I want to get out there and get good stories too. Anyway, keep me posted and I'll keep the powers that be in the know. Mr. Gates told me to reach to him at any time of day or night if anything breaks."

"I'll be in touch. I need to get going. No news yet, but I hope to have something for you tomorrow."

Danica hung up before Hailey could continue any more of their conversation. Hailey was twenty-five, the age she herself was when she started working at DCCC Media Enterprises, the original name of Jason's media empire. She had been as eager to succeed as Hailey is now. That has also been the age that she'd first met Jason. A few years later, the flirting began and then the affair. That had been a huge mistake on her part. She was wondering if she was on the edge of another big mistake. The problem was, could the mistake be that she was lying about who she was to get the scoop on Edrick or was it that she was falling for him and that could lead to disaster? She'd been here before and made the wrong choice all in the name of career advancement for herself.

Not giving it anymore thought, she stood and went to unpack her luggage. She had already planned for at least a week in Spain, so she had plenty of clothes. It was time for her to find something sexy to wear to her dinner with Edrick in a few hours. She would make sure to add her miniature recorder to her purse to capture everything they talked about just in case she couldn't remember it herself. The network was counting on her to come through for them. She was glad that this second chance was coming her way with the faith and support of her leadership. She looked forward to being able to sit across from Marilyn and David, the other morning talk show host, and finally get her chance to prove what she could do if she were given the opportunity to be front and center. She had to come through. They were coming through for her.

**

Hailey stood from Danica's desk at the network and walked up the steps to Warren's office three flights up. With Danica out of town, she loved the feel of being behind her desk. Her own little desk in the outer office where other support staff sat was beneath her. A spacious office like Danica's is exactly where she belonged; it was what she was working for.

Climbing the stairs in her Nike Air Max sneakers, she thanked her trainer for keeping her in shape and for reminding her that steps were better than taking elevators. Happy she had her sneakers on while still in her business suit, she rushed up the steps while adjusting her blouse by opening two extra buttons on her top. She knew how much Warren loved looking at her. When she shared more skin, that was even better. She was using what she had to get what she wanted. Danica may be the one traveling to get the good story, but she was working on her own angle to take the credit and the spotlight away from her.

Exiting on the floor with the executive wing, she waved through the large glass wall of her boss's office. He waved her in as she ignored his secretary who stood to announce her before she rushed in. Hailey loved that she was already developing her own connection with Warren, something his secretary hated.

"I got this," Hailey said to the woman who rolled her eyes and went back to her desk.

"Hailey! Any word from Danica? I assume that's why you're here," he said the minute she walked in. She also greeted Marilyn, who was sitting on the long black leather sofa against the one solid wall in his office.

"I hope she has some news. I'm already prepping the perfect outfit for the day I break the story to our audience. We are going to get to the grit of how Edrick was able to make a million dollars his first year working on the stock market. He was what, twenty-five? That's young. He isn't the Wolf of Wallstreet. Any news?" Marilyn also asked.

Hailey loved that movie the hunky starring Leonardo DiCaprio. It was her favorite. Marilyn making reference to it meant that she hadn't seen the movie. It's about a true story which proved people that young could be that successful. She expected that kind of absent-mindedness from someone her age who only focused on herself and not what was going on around her. She couldn't wait to replace her one day. She smiled at them both and gave her update.

"Nothing yet. There is a huge snow storm. What was to be a short layover in Denver has turned into a possible week-long stay there. Don't worry, Edrick Stone is staying as well. She was able to connect with him to the point that he asked her out for dinner. That's something, right?" she asked, looking between them hoping for a kudo.

"That's Danica – is how you should have said that. I knew we could count on her to relive her past to get what she needs. Wasn't it around this time of year that her life was put on display in the worse way? I remember her saying she didn't mind working the holiday because she hated Christmas anyway," Marilyn noted.

Warren snickered and placed his feet up on his desk, crossing them at the ankles.

"That little lady is about to improve our ratings with this story. This Stone fella has something he's hiding. Everyone takes it easy on him because of his wife and son dying and all. I just want the story; I want the dirt. I know there is some. Danica was the perfect person to go after this for us. Her beauty, brains and desire to be on top will work in our favor," Warren said.

"Think she'll do whatever it takes to get the job done?" Marilyn asked.

"Oh, she'll do it or I'll fire her immediately. The only reason I hired her was to get this story. I knew she was desperate to get ahead after that scandal rocked her world. It's taken all this time for her to get anything that wasn't writing fluff pieces on Hollywood spoiled brats. This is her ticket, or so she thinks. She's got her eye on one of those prize seats at the anchor desk," Warren shared.

Hailey couldn't wait to get her next words out.

"I think she has her eye on your seat, Marilyn. She all but told me that. She thinks it's time for you to move on. I, on the other hand, would love to be able to learn from you, the master at the journalist game," Hailey lied.

"I thought you liked working for her," Marilyn said.

"Oh, I do, I do. I don't have a goal of unseating anyone to get ahead."

"Well, she's not unseating me. That's my seat until I say otherwise. She better remember that. She better not mess this up for us. There is a lot riding on getting the dirt on him. If she wins, we all win. If she loses, she loses on her own. She better remember I said by any means necessary. She's used to sleeping her way to the top. Let's see if she's willing to do that for a win this time. I'm not a fan of keeping her on board anyway. We can't have her around here potentially ruining careers because she can't tell the difference between lust and love," Warren joked.

"Yeah. Jason never really recovered. Bad for him, but good for us. He could have been a serious rival for our network if his life hadn't crashed and burned. The wife got half and that company was never the same. He tried to re-brand but it never took off. I hear he's now living in the South of France with a new wife. He took his money and disappeared from the spotlight. Meanwhile, Danica has tried for years to get her foot in the door anywhere," Marilyn explained.

"She was given a chance, but I'm a little shaky on her real potential. We'll see if she comes through. Hailey, stay on top of this. I want to know about anything she uncovers so that we can get people on this to dive even deeper."

"Yes, sir, I will."

Hailey nodded to them both and left the office. She was already working to put her plan in place. She was even willing to give up her Christmas plans to stay close to the office knowing how big the story could be for them if it was true. So far, she hadn't been able to find anything negative on Edrick when she began digging into him herself. She was hoping Danica would and then she'd use that to push Danica out of the way. She couldn't wait.

4

Edrick opened the door to his suite and quickly pulled his best friend into a hug.

"Bro! I still can't believe you're here!" Albert shouted as he entered.

Edrick nodded having the same thought. He had been kicking himself for thinking about passing through Denver and not contacting him and Misha, especially this time of year. If no one else knew where his mind was, Albert would. That's why he wasn't angry knowing that this meet and greet wouldn't have happened if it had not been for the snow storm.

"I know, me either. I'm glad you could take some time from your crazy schedule to stop in for a drink. I will say that going overboard on the Christmas decorations in my suite is a bit much. Does everyone's room look like this? Who had time to decorate every room along with the open resort space at this level? Your wife is amazing," he laughed.

"You know how she is. It's all about the experience for her," Albert explained.

"I thought we were going to meet in one of the bars or the casino. This resort is the last word! I can't wait to get a tour of it all. This one is bigger and better than what you already have."

"I would have sent you an invite for the grand opening early next year, in February. We've already completely booked up this place around Valentine's Day. I wasn't sure you wanted to be here for that, but for the ribbon cutting, your invitation was on the way," Albert explained. "If it wasn't for you and your financial guidance, I wouldn't have any of this," he added.

Edrick followed Albert further into the grand suite to the kitchen. It was complete with everything a kitchen in a mansion would have. He saw the bottles of beer in Albert's hands and couldn't wait to dive in. After two of the six bottles were opened and Albert handed one to him, Edrick took a seat at the gray and white marble island that could set four on each side of it. The suite was more like an apartment than a provision at a hotel.

"This place is crazy nice."

"Yeah? You like how we put you up? You know you only get the best from us, right?"

"I know and I appreciate it. Do you really leave my old spot open for me every year? You don't lease it out?" Edrick asked.

There was a time that he and Phaedra loved what was their suite whenever they traveled to Denver. Being friends with Albert since high school, his best friend had married the woman of his dreams and made a great life for them in the mountains of Colorado.

"I had to or Misha would have my head. You know how she is about you; a good friend I've had since we were what, fifteen or sixteen?"

"Right. We met in the tenth grade, Ms. Shadow's class at Walter Mason High School."

"Yes, the sexist math teacher to ever walk the planet. Man, I couldn't wait to get to school to be in her first period class. I had her again in our senior year for Trigonometry. She was my first big crush," Albert admitted.

"Man, she was every guy's first big crush. She was beautiful. Not as beautiful as Misha, but yeah, beautiful."

"I still can't believe I'm married to her. How are you really doing? I know you didn't plan on being here for Christmas. This is the fifth year?" Albert asked.

Edrick couldn't believe it's been five years already.

"Christian would have been ten years old. The struggle is still real," Edrick explained.

"I hope you're not continuing to blame yourself for what happened. You couldn't have stopped that accident or their deaths."

If it were anyone else, he would change the subject. With Albert, nothing was ever off limits when it came to them catching up.

"I know, but maybe if I was driving, it would not have happened. Phaedra wanted me to join them in Honduras early for the opening of the school. She was all about helping the underprivileged and the undeserved get what they need in order to live successful lives. Her mission work is what made me love her even more. She loved helping others. I should have been there. You know I hustled hard every day not to gain wealth for me, but to earn it so that she could open up every school she wanted to around the world. Like Oprah, she had big plans to bring education to Africa. She still had so much to do. I still struggle with this being my life. This is what Christmas will forever mean for me."

"Don't keep carrying this weight around. You need to find a purpose to love Christmas again. You remember how much Phaedra loved coming here a week before Christmas each year to help Misha get the resort all decorated and ready for the holiday. She loved Christmas. Christian would look at all of the decorations with those big dark gray eyes and red curly hair. She even convinced you a few times to dress up as Santa for the kids. This was a place of fun and happiness. I wish I could make this time of year a happy one for you again."

Edrick nodded, afraid to speak knowing he would get choked up remembering how much his son loved Christmas. He missed them and he missed being in Denver for Christmas. Thankfully, this year, fate played a hand in the decision of where he would spend it.

"I promise to not bring everyone down. I'm happy to be here."

"Would all this happiness have anything to do with that beautiful woman in purple that I saw you catering to and laughing with when you arrived? You were completely focused on her and what she needed. When I saw you walk into the lobby smiling like a high school kid happy that the most popular cheerleader was giving him attention, I didn't know what was going on. You're usually so somber this time of year, but there you were, all smiles."

"She's a nice woman I met on the plane. We were both in first class sitting across the aisle from each other. I liked talking to her," Edrick admitted.

"And looking at her. She's gorgeous. It's okay to admit that to me. I'm your best friend and I won't judge."

Edrick took another swig of his beer to buy himself some time to either give off an admission or figure out a way to dismiss the idea.

"Yes, at to look at because look at her; she's stunning. I don't usually get too into a conversation with a woman beyond enough chatter to get us to a bed someplace. I won't apologize for that. You know my heart has been on lockdown since the accident. There was something about Danica when I was talking to her that gave me a level of comfort I haven't experienced in a long time."

"Not since Phaedra?" Albert asked pointedly.

Edrick wanted to say that. He'd been thinking it himself. The issue was, he didn't know what it meant. Maybe it was the lull of the holiday spirit. Perhaps he was finally coming out of his funk about the Christmas holiday. All he knew was that if it weren't for the layover in Denver, he wouldn't be getting ready to have dinner with her in a few hours.

"I don't know how to answer that. All that I can say is that I like her. It was only a two-and-a-half-hour flight. That has to be some kind of record for falling for a woman," Edrick laughed.

Did he just say that? Did he really just admit that he was more into Danica than he expected to be? This feeling truly was a first for him.

"Maybe Santa is trying to get back into your good graces again. Listen, whatever it is, I'm just happy I saw you smile like that. It's been a while, my friend. How is business?"

"Business is great. I was in Seattle meeting with new clients who were the sons of a client who recently passed away. Their father left everything to them and to my surprise, they didn't just want to take the money, liquidate all the assets and run. They want me to work with them on trading and investing a large portion of their wealth. I had my team from my New York office in Seattle with me to get the ball rolling with contract signing and all of that. That was a few days ago. I stayed a few extra days and got caught in the storm."

"I see you still doing big things. Mr. Hilliard set you up right. You were always brilliant with numbers. I still remember the day Ms. Shadow let you teach our math class. Then when we got to college and you had your first math class with Mr. Hilliard, he immediately saw your savvy with numbers."

"I sure do miss him. He died way too soon. I'm glad he was able to see that his teaching and coaching me in how to let numbers make me a rich man had actually paid off. He was able to see that I was listening. He taught me everything I know about the stock market, trading, investing, asset management."

"Numbers were always going to be your ticket. You said that at one time, the Feds were looking into how you made your wealth and determined you were legit."

Edrick hated thinking about that. It seemed the more money he made, the more government agencies came after him. Thankfully, he had the best legal minds in the world who counseled him well. He had nothing to hide, so he let them in. Still, the experience was annoying. Her persevered in spite of.

"They never expected to see a black man in that kind of money game without there being some kind of illegal edge to it. In fact, not just a black man, but any man. I opened up all of my books to them and in no time, they realized it was all good. You've been scrutinized also because of our connection to me and how you've succeeded in business."

"Yeah, I never lost any sleep over that, just like you didn't. They were more interested in whether I thought you were stealing from me, though you were also making me rich. They didn't recognize that we were created to survive. Now, about this week. Are you staying the whole week or will you be sneaking off to Spain in the middle of the night?"

Edrick laughed out loud. This is why he missed hanging with Albert. He never shied away from the hard questions.

"I'm here for the week. Actually, I was going to leave when flights out were allowed again, but then, I asked Danica if she'd like to consider staying and enjoying the festivities and amenities. We're having dinner in a few hours."

Edrick looked away and took a gulp of his beer. He already knew that Albert would have a big, stupid grin on his face.

"I'm telling you, it's Santa at work. The Christmas spirit is flowing back into your life. I couldn't be happier. Wait until Misha hears there is a woman you have your eye on. Maybe we can connect and have lunch in the casino tomorrow. Bring Danica with you if she'd like to come. I'd want to meet her."

"Now, hold your horses. We're not dating or anything. It's just dinner. Like I said, she was a delight to talk to and because of the extended layover, we'll get a chance to really sit and talk."

"If you say so, I'll go with that. Still, Misha and I try to take time in the middle of the day to sit and relax. She loves the food at the casino because the chef is from Baltimore. He also provides dinner in the main restaurant and club."

"That's where we're having dinner at tonight."

"You'll love it. You know how much Misha loves seafood, so that's the place to be if you want fantastic crab cakes. The chef won some recent cooking show. We were able to get him under contract with a split in the profits. He brings it along with all of his seafood creations. Think about it and let me know. I need to say again how happy I am that you're here. I know the circumstances aren't idea. Just remember, you are always welcome here. From this time forward, we'll make this new suite your home away from home and go back to leasing out the old space. Misha has been sentimental but maybe it's time we all moved on."

"Yeah, you're right about that."

"Let me also say that it's time to move on in many ways. Look, we have a million activities planned that are all fun. I've already had the itinerary sent to your email. Check it out. I know you'll be down for some poker later this week. Relax, enjoy yourself and remember that Christmas is just a holiday. It's the family and friends that matter. How are your parents doing?" Albert asked.

Edrick smiled from ear to ear at the thought of Brenda and Maxwell Stone. The best day of his life was when he was able to retire both of them. His mother has dived into philanthropy, taking over the great work that Phaedra had been doing to help the less fortunate. His father, who sat on the board of the non-profit that oversaw the work, loved what he was doing. To him, it's a lot less stressful than the life he lived running a construction company. They were able to do what they wanted to do and when they wanted to do it. Like Albert, they tried to pull him out of his slump around this time of year. Luckily, he escaped their pressure this year with their vacation.

"Man, they are living the life. My mother oversaw the opening of a school for boys and young men in Africa. My dad joined her and they turned the end of that trip into a two-week vacation on a cruise ship. They were going to visit me in Spain, not wanting me to sit around and sulk, but I convinced them that I would be okay. See, I am. I'm here with you in Denver, I'm about to have dinner with a beautiful woman and this year, Christmas isn't so bad after all."

"That's what I want to hear. I say it's the woman, but I won't force you to admit it. Listen, you have a few minutes to chat about work? I want to talk about some new stocks to invest in with the extra profits we're making from the resorts."

"I'm always up for talking about money. Let me get my laptop and let's talk. I have a few hours before I have to meet Danica."

Edrick stood to leave the kitchen.

"Beautiful name for a beautiful woman. I hope she turns out to be worthy of more than dinner."

Albert spoke to his back and Edrick stiffened.

"From your lips, bro. That's all I'm going to say."

What he wanted to say but didn't was that he hoped Danica could be more than just a dinner date. There was something about her that he couldn't shake. Maybe Santa was reminding him that love at Christmas time was okay.

"Love?" Edrick questioned out loud without meaning to.

"What?" Albert asked.

Edrick grumbled. That had slipped out. There was no way he was thinking of being in love with anyone, especially not with a woman he'd met earlier in the day. No way, he thought, grabbing his computer.

He needed to remember to call his housekeeper in Spain to let her know to keep his house locked up and to enjoy her holiday. He was glad that he'd given her the Christmas bonus he couldn't wait to give her each year. She would be at his house preparing for him to come home. He was happily staying in a place that did bring happy memories. And for now, maybe even the chance for some new memories to be made. Only time will tell.

5

With the knock on her hotel room door, Danica rushed toward it. Feeling too anxious for what she didn't even know was a date or not, she stopped and slowed herself down. She needed to contain her nervousness before she opened the door to the man she'd been unable to stop thinking about all day.

After picking out the perfect dress in red to match the holiday atmosphere, she loved how sexy the long sleeved, velvet wrap dress made her feel. She was glad she remembered to pack it. She had no idea she'd be wearing it to a dinner date with a handsome man like Edrick. Taking less rushed steps, she grabbed her small silver bag which matched her strappy silver slingback heels to be sure she had something to put her room key in. Working to control her rapidly beating heart, she opened the door. On the other side of it, Edrick was leaning against the door frame dressed in all black. She checked him out from the floor up. He was stimulatingly sexy in his business attire earlier, but now, with this more casual look, her heart skipped a few beats. There would be no controlling her reaction to him tonight.

Seeing him in a black buttoned-down shirt with matching slacks with a platinum watch on his wrist and a thick link platinum chain on his other wrist, he was giving her all kinds of man-model type vibes. His full beard was freshly trimmed along with his mustache. The bald head thing he had going on only added to his attractiveness. He reminded her of the actor, D. B. Woodside, who played Melvin "Blue" Franklin in the Temptations movie. Their features were similar.

"Wow," she said without thinking first. The rage within her came to the surface at being this forward. Being embarrassed was new to her, but here she was, looking into his eyes. His awareness of her level of discomfort after that outburst didn't turn him off. To her liking, he smiled, reassuring her that her comment was not out of line.

"I'll take that as a compliment," he said. "Or maybe not?" he added.

Danica knew he was joking with that quirky grin on his face.

"A compliment, indeed," she said.

"You are a showstopper in that dress. You are a very beautiful woman, Danica. I need to get that out of the way before we get to dinner. Red is definitely your color. In fact, I bet every color is your color. I remember how your purple coat on the plane brought out the hazel flecks in your light brown eyes. Absolutely stunning. Are you ready? I can't wait for heads to turn when I walk into dinner with you," Edrick said.

Danica went from being embarrassed to a blushing mass of delight.

"I'm glad you like and yes, I'm ready."

Letting the door shut and lock behind her, she matched his stride as they walked toward the elevator.

"How do you like the hotel? Is your suite okay?" Edrick asked when he pushed the elevator button.

"I love everything about the hotel. My suite is made for a queen. I had no idea this place existed," she said as the elevator doors opened and they stepped in.

"Really? You're not too far since you live in Seattle. I can't believe you've never heard of this place or been here before. Most people on the west coast frequent the resort. It's the largest and most popular in the state. Nothing compares."

Danica turned her head away from Edrick's view and lightly bit her lower lip. She slipped up again. She forgot that she is supposed to be from Seattle and not from the east coast. She needed to save herself.

"I do a lot of traveling to the east coast more than I do the west coast. I like the weather on that side of the country better. I will definitely make sure this isn't my last stay here. Tomorrow, I've signed up for a few spa treatments. There is so much to do. Since I'll be here for about a week, I want to see and do some things."

"Are you still going to allow me to show you around? Recommend some of the best amenities?"

He still wanted to do that. She thought that perhaps, he'd forgotten that he offered to be her guide for the week. She was excited knowing that he still wanted to.

"I look forward to it. I didn't think you remembered that you had offered."

"What? Forget about being in the company of a beautiful woman? No way. I'm in if you are," he said.

"I don't want to take up all of your time. Hey, what floor are you on? Is your room nice?" she asked.

"I'm on the top floor in what they call a grand suite. It is amazing. Misha and Albert always roll out the red carpet for me. They've been doing that for years since they opened their first resort six or seven years ago."

"Wow. They've accumulated all of this in that short period of time? They must have a great financial planner. It must take a lot to continually build on top of what they have."

There. She put the idea of finances into the atmosphere. She only had to wait to see if he would bite. As fine as he was, she was here to work.

"That would be me," Edrick responded in kind as they entered the restaurant. Danica stood in amazement at the staff who ran up to greet Edrick as if he was a long-lost family member. It was clear that he was well-known.

"Mr. Stone, it's so good to see you back on the mountain. It's been too long," one man said.

"Horace, I thought you worked at the *Bennie Resort*, the first location Albert established," Edrick addressed.

"I was. Mr. London gave those of us who have been here a long time the option to come work at the new spot. I jumped right on it. I'm the maître d here now. I have the perfect table already set up for you."

"I take it Albert told you I was coming?" Edrick asked.

Danica felt a shiver in her body when they were being escorted to their table and Edrick guided her to the space in front of him by placing his hand lightly in the center of her back. That little touch had her on fire. She smiled and blushed all at the same time.

"No, sir. Mrs. London gave specific instructions to seat you at our best and to make sure the chef prepares whatever you want even if it's not on the list of specials for the night," Horace said.

Danica nodded as Edrick pulled out her chair before taking the seat across from her.

"I won't be much trouble, Horace. I'm sure everything on the menu is delicious and will be fine for us," Edrick responded.

"Very good, sir. The wine list is here. Someone will be over shortly to see what you would like to start with. I know Mr. London is all kinds of happy you are here."

"I'm happy to be here, too."

After Horace walked away, Danica finally leaned over to talk directly to him.

"How much time did you used to spend here? Everyone speaks and greets you like you're their brother from another mother," she delighted in saying.

"In a way, I am. Albert and I have been best friends since high school. I used to spend this week here every single year, but not so much anymore. I would also come for a week-long summer festival he hosts each year. Entertainment is performed by the best of the best in the music industry. Every room, villa, chalet and cabin are booked solid for that week of nothing but great fun, food and music. You've never heard of that either?" he asked.

"I guess I live a sheltered life," she said.

Danica wanted to drive the conversation back to how he was Albert's money guy.

"Sounds like it. You need to live more. Come to think of it, a lot of my winter months were spent here. I love to ski."

"I'm here for a week and we're getting snowed in, so I guess I will learn to live more, thanks to you," she replied and smiled. "You mentioned you were the finance person behind Albert's success or something to that affect. Is that so?"

"Oh, right, we were talking about that on the elevator. I'm an investment counselor, asset and money manager, stock trader – you name it. I help others get and maintain their wealth when it comes to investing. I'm been blessed to be an expert in that. I have several investment houses and brokerage firms across the United States. I also have six others in various countries around the world. I'm a numbers guy."

"Ah, and being Albert's best friend, you help him stay as well off as you, I'm sure are. That's the kind of friends I need. Most of mine always want to borrow money."

Danica was joking while also being serious at the same time.

"Those friends need to learn how to save and invest. It's the American way."

"But you're no longer American, right? You mentioned you live in Spain?"

"I do, but I'm still an American citizen. I was born and raised here. I happen to have homes in several locations. I love the privacy I get when I'm in Spain. It's all home to me. I would never give up my citizenship here. I love it too much."

Just then their waitress showed up to the table. They ordered drinks and several appetizers.

Before their conversation resumed, a very beautiful woman with skin the color of mocha and hair as black and shining as coal took to the stage to the applause of many.

"Is she going to sing?" she asked Edrick.

When he laughed, she cut her eyes his way.

"Not in this lifetime. That's Misha, Albert's wife. I'm sure she's about to announce whoever the entertainment is for the night. Albert recently began a residency of artists here at the resort. There is a long list of artists waiting to get in on the action. Wait until you see who is here tonight," Edrick said and pointed for her to look back at the stage.

"Ladies and gentlemen. There is no need for a huge introduction of our esteemed songstress for this week. You can find her here each night bringing you the best in R&B. Let's all salute, the queen of hip hop soul, the one and only, Mary J. Blige!" Misha yelled.

Danica couldn't believe what her ears just heard. Could it really be that her favorite singer of all time was here at the resort while she was here? Was this about to be her best Christmas *ever*? She stood along with everyone else when a vision in a red long, beaded gown with a split up the side revealing a lot of leg walked out along with a harpist, a guitar player and a single piano player. Her hair was up and she was draped in enough diamonds that a jeweler with security must have been nearby to protect all that glitz.

The cheers throughout the crowd that had to be well over two hundred were so loud that Danica could barely hear her own cheers and hoops. When she turned and looked at Edrick, he was still as calm and collected as he has been since the moment they met. What caught her attention was that his eyes were not on the stage and the woman who was about to sing; his eyes were on her. For a few seconds, she stopped clapping and cheering and kept her eyes locked on his. There was an unspoken connection that said their night was just beginning. She couldn't look away. Everything about him was pulling her in. She refused to let the hold that had developed over each other go. She knew about him only what she's seen in the reports her assistant had provided. At this moment, none of that mattered. If she thought she felt something for him on the plane and when they sat next to each other on the ride to the resort, she knew for sure in the way he was looking at her that something was happening between the two of them. It was unexpected and shocked her to her core.

She felt his desire for her in his gaze, which she knew matched her own. His heated stare was overpowering. She was losing her resolve and the guard she had up to protect her heart and focus on her reason for being with him. One thing she knew for sure, she was a goner.

Finally, looking away and back at Mary J. Blige, Danica quivered at the thought of being the true object of his desire in a more private setting. She knew she shouldn't let her mind go there, but she couldn't help herself. In a few short hours, she was on the precipice of just going with the flow. If his eyes were relaying what his mind was thinking, the fire she saw in them was all the invitation she needed and wanted.

Tuning that out for now, she returned to focus on the stage when Mary began singing. This was officially the best Christmas holiday of her life. Hot man admiring her, her favorite singer about to belt out all of her favorites and from the menu, she was about to partake in some delicious delicacies.

When the music began, she finally sat back down and turned back to Edrick.

"Impressed?" he asked her.

"More than you know."

Danica meant more than just the entertainment. What was it about this man that had her operating outside of herself? She was still remembering making a mistake years ago combining work and pleasure. It didn't work out well for her then. Something was telling her it wasn't going to work out for her now either. She needed to make a choice. It was a hard one, but it needed to be made.

"Oh, I do know, trust me. Would you like to dance?" he asked, catching her off-guard.

"Dance? You dance?" she asked.

"Doesn't everyone?"

Edrick stood and offered her his hand just as Mary began to croon one of her favorite songs, *Seven Days*. How perfect was the moment and the song?

"I didn't know she would sing a slow song. We can wait if you like," Edrick offered.

Danica didn't want to wait. She wanted to dance now; to this song. Nothing prepared her for this moment of recognition. They desired each other; just like that. It was happening to her. At least this time, she wasn't falling for a man who belonged to another woman. That much she was able to find out from her research.

Not giving it a second thought, Danica placed her hand in his and stood. She followed him to the dance floor where she hoped he'd hold her close. When Edrick turned and invited her into his arms, she went without hesitation knowing she had just been wishing for that.

The moment his arms went around her waist, she raised her arms and rested them at his shoulders. With him, well over six feet tall, she had to tilt her head up, even in five-inch heels, to look into his eyes. His gaze was magnetic; even mesmerizing. The longing she saw in them didn't surprise her because she knew he was seeing the same in her eyes. Was it this easy? Could she have fallen for a man she was supposed to be digging up information on? Could she separate the two? Perhaps she could have this one night of not thinking about work and just enjoy the moment. That's why she accepted his invitation to dinner. It wasn't about the job; it was about the man. He felt so good in her arms. The way they swayed to the music was enchanted. Edrick leaned close to her ear. She turned her head sideways to give him room.

"You are truly one of the most beautiful women I have ever had the pleasure of having in my arms on the dance floor. I wanted you to know that. I'm not saying it to gain anything. I'm saying it because it's true. If that's too much, let me know. That's not my intent," he whispered.

Danica gulped down the huge lump in her throat. Never, ever had a man made her feel this desirable – and she meant *never*.

"Thank you, Edrick. Thank you for making me feel beautiful."

"Anytime," he said.

In the next moment, all bets were off when it came to work and she knew it. Edrick began humming to the song as the words cascaded out of his mouth like her very own serenade. The man was hot, sexy, intelligent and carried confidence like none she'd ever met. On top of that, he could sing. She was a lost cause and she knew it. Her only thought as she laid her head on his chest and enjoyed the moment was how would her night end? She knew how she would like for it to end, but she didn't know what Edrick was thinking. She wanted to go with the moment and forget about any task she had to complete for work. She wanted Edrick.

As they danced, she wondered if it was the song, the atmosphere, the festive holiday season or what seemed to be a romantic environment that had her feeling like she and Edrick could be more. Were her thoughts going to get her from the frying pan and into the fire? She'd been there before. It wasn't a pleasant experience. In fact, she would give her past experience zero stars; she would not recommend it. But this, a sudden rush of desire for Edrick, she would recommend to everyone. It wasn't anything in particular that he said; it was who he was.

Danica could hear his heart beating through his shirt. It wasn't rushed or racing, but calm and soothing. He was comfortable with her; as comfortable as she was with him.

Before too long, the song ended and they saw their appetizers being set up on their table. Putting her hand in his once again, Edrick guided them through other dancers where they sat and placed their dinner orders before diving into the best-looking shrimp cocktail, antipasto skewers and crab cake poppers. She ordered smothered chicken over sauteed veggies and potatoes and grilled green beans. Edrick ordered blackened salmon, maple glazed brussels sprouts and mashed turnips. They were ready for a feast.

"You know, I'm not a big fan of Christmas," she admitted.

That wasn't a lie crafted by her assistant. This was her being totally truthful.

"You are not the only one. Maybe that's why we connected. The only kind of people who run away from being with family for Christmas are those who aren't fans of the holiday. I hope whatever tarnished your love for Christmas has you seeing it in a better light."

Danica nodded.

Merry Christmas to me, she thought to herself.

"That it has. It started with that first hello from you when I got entered the plane."

Danica was being all kinds of honest-like. She still had secrets but who she was giving him now is what she was truly about.

"That's interesting because before I said hello to you, my disdain for this holiday was epic. I lost my wife and son on Christmas Eve five years ago."

Danica's back stiffened. Could Edrick have been going through his own misery while she was going through hers? She knew what had happened to his family, but she hadn't paid a lot of attention to the date. It was five years ago for her, one night away too, to Christmas Eve when the world found out about her affair.

"I'm sorry to hear that. Do you mind sharing or is that prying? I don't mean to," she admitted, and once again, meant it.

"I don't mind at all. My wife, Phaedra and our five-year-old son, Christian were in Honduras on a mission's trip to finally open up a school she had been overseeing the construction of for over a year. I was going to bring Christian with me and join her on Christmas day, but I had some important business deals that I needed to close out before the end of the year. She decided to take Christian with her to allow me the time to get my work done and then join them. On Christmas Eve, she was making one last ride out to check on the school and it appears she lost control of the jeep they were riding it. It went over an embankment, rolling over and over onto the rocks below, killing both of them on impact. That started my hatred for Christmas, which is why I was on my way to Spain to spend the season alone. I've been doing that since they died. I would still be doing everything I could to get there, but then I met you on the plane this morning. There was something about you. Then there was the delay right here in Denver where my best friend owns a resort. Things just seemed to fall into place for me to go in a different direction. I went with a feeling in my gut that said I shouldn't walk away from the most dynamic woman I've encountered in a long time. I went with it. Is that too much?" he asked.

Danica's heart melted and hurt for him. The loss of a wife and child had to have been devastating. The story she read was nothing compared to hearing him tell it to her himself. His words were filled with emotion which was lacking in the words of the report she'd read.

She remembered reading the stories about the accident and the aftermath. It turns out there was a mechanical issue with the jeep. The settlement Edrick received was never shared with the public. She heard that he donated it all in the name of his wife and son to the school whose name was changed to be named after the two of them. Now, her life choice of getting involved with a married man and having it all fall apart seemed minor to what happened to him. How is it that they had disasters on the same day, years ago and then now, connect in such a magical way on a plane? Something else was at work and it wasn't by her hands or Edrick's.

"Not at all. I'm so sorry for your loss."

"What made you hate the holiday?" he asked.

"Nothing like what happened to you. For me, it was about making bad choices and having them come back to haunt me. I'm happy knowing that those feelings of dread around Christmas don't last always. I can honestly say that this Christmas layover has been the best Christmas ever for me."

"I'm with you on that. Maybe after dinner we could check out the movie theater and see what's playing. I'm not ready for the night to end yet. I know it just started with dinner and the concert. I already know I'll feel this way when we're done here."

"You have all kinds of energy, huh? There's a movie theater around here?" she asked.

"There is a theater right here in this resort. In fact, there are three movie screens in the theater. If it's the same as the other resorts, some of the best buttered popcorn around is included."

"I'm definitely in."

Danica was so excited as she swooned to the music and the delectable taste of her appetizers that everything other than the man across from her vanished from her psyche. She didn't care about work. She didn't care about anything other than how happy she was knowing that the night would not end with dinner. There was more in store and she was ready. She was on a date and if she was lucky, it would be one that will last well into the next day. Tomorrow was Christmas Eve and she couldn't wait to get to it.

**

Edrick thought after dinner, the concert and a movie that he would be ready to turn Danica loose for the evening. As they exited the movie theater to head toward her room, he could not have been more wrong. Reaching the elevator, he pushed the button that would take them to her floor. With her shoes, connected together by the straps, in one of his hands and her hand in the other, he was hoping the elevator would take a long time.

After dinner and staying until Mary J. had sung her last song, they walked hand-in-hand to the onsite movie theater. Two of the movies playing were Christmas holiday classics and another was the latest Tom Cruise movie. They opted for one of the Christmas movies, *Miracle on 34th Street*, a movie they both remembered watching as kids. Edrick enjoyed every moment of being with Danica. It was as if they hadn't just met but had known each other for much longer. Before too long, the movie ended and with it being after midnight, it was time for the night to end. He knew it but he didn't have to like it.

"One of the best nights of my life," he shared.

"Looks like great minds are thinking alike again. I was really thinking the same thing. I can't believe I enjoyed that movie as if I was watching it for the first time. I can never lose my excitement over watching that little girl run throughout that house knowing it was the exact one she had asked Santa for."

"And when they saw Kris Kringle's cane leaning against the wall? One of the best holiday movies ever. Too bad it wasn't a four- or five-hour movie."

Danica looked at him perplexed. Edrick knew he was going to have to explain himself.

"Why?" she asked.

"Because that would mean I wouldn't have to say good night to you in a few minutes. I'm having a good time and not quite ready to walk away from you."

"Me either."

Danica replied so fast, Edrick didn't know what to say. His eyes captured hers. He knew the look. Before he could respond, the elevator doors opened and they got in. When he reached to push the button for her floor, six, Danica reached for his hand and stopped him. She then reached to the panel and instead of hitting six, she hit twenty, the top floor of the resort where he told her his suite was.

When the doors closed, an overwhelming sensation to hold her became the priority of the moment. Ever since the moment she opened her door to him and he saw her standing before him like a woman out of his dream, he'd been thinking about what her red covered lips tasted like. He hoped he was about to find out.

He pulled her into his arms knowing that the moment didn't call for words; it called for an intoxicating kiss that he hoped would douse the powerful craving he had for her. Taking his time to allow her the chance to pull away if she didn't want what he did, he lifted her chin and gazed into her smoldering eyes. He captured her lips like a hungry man; gentle but intentional. When she returned the kiss with as much fervor as him, his brain did a happy dance that he'd made the right decision.

Edrick dipped her head back and when her lips parted under his with a plea for more, he gave her what she sought and what he needed. His need for more of her was unwavering as he moved them to the back of the elevator, pulling her body flush against his. There was no doubt that she could feel his desire for her growing as the elevator moved closer to their destination. He wasn't shy about his need for more of her; for all of her. Leaning back, he looked for any signs of doubt on her face and saw none.

Danica's eyes sparkled with awareness. He needed to know that she was enjoying the moment as much as he was. He saw it plain and clear. What was next for them wasn't as clear; it was unspoken. They were simply acting on what they believed her choosing his floor over hers meant.

"Are you sure?" he asked. He needed to know. He would turn back if he had to, but he didn't want to.

"I've never, ever been surer of anything in my life. Are you sure?" she returned his very question back to him.

Edrick smiled, kissed her one last time with the sweetest touch of his lips and then found his way to her ear.

"I am as sure as sure can get. I've been sure about wanting you since you got on that plane. It may not have been evident at that time."

Danica moved closer to him; the evidence quite clear.

"If it wasn't evident then, it is now," she declared. To bring her point home, Edrick watched her eyes lower to the space between them where his desire was quite evident. "You're not alone at all. I'm ready. I want this; I want you," she said, convincing him. He heard the words. He felt the yearning.

When the doors opened on his floor, Edrick took her hand in his again as they walked to his room. With each step, his heart pounded relentlessly in his chest. Taking a woman to bed after meeting her wasn't new to him. He'd been doing just that for the past few years. What was new was the fact that Danica is the first woman that he wanted to see again in the light of day. He didn't want to disappear like a thief in the night like he had done with other women. He never wanted any of them to feel deserted but he had not been ready for more that what the night called for. With Danica, there was much more he wanted from her and for them.

He'd been wishing that she felt what he felt. Now, he knew.

Edrick wasn't sure if it was a Christmas wish or just a simple old wish. He would take it in any form. He paused at his door and turned to her. He was met with the biggest, brightest smile any woman had ever bestowed on him. He leaned down and kissed her smile.

"No hesitation?" he asked.

"Not from me. I know what will be on the other side. It's why I pushed the button. Now, all you have to do is open the door."

Edrick winked at her.

"Oh, I intend to do that. I want to be clear about something," he started to say before she touched a finger to his lips quieting him.

"Are you going to say you only want this one night?" she asked.

"Not on your life. I was going to say that I don't want this to be only one night. I want to see if something nice can come of us. Are you up for that? I don't think I can handle having you for one night and then walking away. That's not my plan. You?" he asked.

"I'm with you until."

That was all he needed to hear. Edrick opened the door, moved to allow her entrance and closed the door behind them. He suddenly realized it was already Christmas Eve. His life was about to change. He hoped Danica was as ready as he already was. He was going on instinct that their meeting was not by coincidence. It was meant to happen. They were meant to bring each other out of a holiday slump. Remembering to put the do not disturb sign on the other side of the door, he locked it behind them. In the next second, he had Danica in his arms, kissing her passionately. The night was only beginning.

6

Edrick wanted to slow things down between them. As much as he wanted to divest her of every piece of clothing, starting with the sexy red dress that hugged her curvy hips. Everything about her had been slowly seducing him all evening. If that was the purpose, there was a point for Danica in the win column.

Turning her loose to allow his body to calm and not rush them, he leaned back against the door and watched as Danica let her eyes scan the room.

"You were not kidding when you said that your friends laid out the red carpet for you. I think my apartment can fit in this living room. Is the rest of the place as elegant as this? I've never seen this mint shade of green before. It's beautiful. The furniture even blends in the specs of the same color throughout," she admired.

"Go look around if you want to. The entire place is amazing. They outdid themselves with extravagance."

Once Danica walked off, Edrick let go of the deep

breath he'd been holding in. Was he really nervous? If so, this feeling was a first for him. He needed to regroup after a few kisses had practically stolen his breath away. The potency of the wanderlust -filled way in which they went at each other's lips had his body screaming for her.

Moving away from the wall he followed the path Danica had taken. He stopped when he found her standing in the doorway of the master bedroom.

"I love everything about this resort. The rooms have a way of making you feel like home," she whispered with her back to him.

Edrick braced his hands on the door frame and leaned close to her ear. He had to hold onto something before he picked her up and found himself in the center of his bed with his body covering hers. With the night ahead of them still young, his mind raced with every sexy detail of what he wanted to do with her.

"Feel to stop by here at any time. My home away from home can be your home away from home as well."

With his next move, he decided to take a chance. There was no need for either of them to behave as if they weren't on the same page. The skin that covered her shoulders shimmered and called to him. He saw a perfect place for a kiss. Taking the liberty he hoped would be welcomed, Edrick let his lips cascade across her shoulder. He touched her lightly. When Danica inhaled sharply and leaned back against him, cocking her neck to the side to give him even more room, he let his hands slide down her arms. One kiss, two kisses, three and even more. Her skin felt as if it were reaching up to him as he caressed it with his mouth.

Danica saw stars as ripples of pleasure flowed through her. Edrick's lips on her sensitized skin helped lessen the hard feeling of the knot that had formed in her stomach. She wasn't uneasy; she'd never been more aroused than her current state of being. There were so many reasons racing through her head that told her she shouldn't be here. She couldn't turn away. She wanted Edrick. When guilt tried to enter their interaction, she shooed it away. Now wasn't the time for her to struggle with her conscious over whether she was making the right choice or not. She wanted to make the only choice that mattered; she was choosing him. Everything and everyone else be damned.

Danica turned and faced the man responsible for her racing heartbeat, sweating palms and quivering body. She leaned up and kissed him powerfully, pouring her fast-beating heart into every touch, every caress of her tongue until their need to breathe was more than evident. What was also just as clear was that there was no turning back.

Stepping away, she backed up toward the bed, hitting Edrick with intense eye contact that was devoted to letting him know that she came into his bedroom for a reason. The euphoric burn of desire to have him all over her wouldn't and couldn't be dismissed. She needed more; she has since the moment they met on the plane. If she had thought of being hesitant in her need for him, he cured her of that by the way his eyes had her losing all sense of time and space. For tonight, it was only them.

Edrick pressed away from the wall, happy that when he left to join her for dinner earlier, he'd left a small light on in the room. That and the bright starry night outside of the window added a glow to Danica's beauty. She was an appearance from a wish he didn't know he'd made. He felt the flutters in his stomach the closer he moved to her. Without any pretense, he reached down and pulled his shirt up over his head and let it land on the floor, not caring where. When he saw Danica reaching for the zipper on the side of her dress, he reached for her hands and stopped her.

"Let me, please," he uttered.

Danica wasn't sure she was still breathing. Her body was on fire, reacting lucidly to the melodic sound of his deep lustful voice. Her body pleaded with anticipation of what was to come. She was all his. With her hands on the softness on the comforter, she followed his eyes as his gaze drifted slowly down her body and back up to land on her breasts. She could feel the sensitive tips as they brushed to pointed peaks inside of the lacy cups of her bra.

Edrick kicked off his shoes and moved to his knees in the center of her legs. His eyes never wavered and neither did hers. Placing his head between her breasts, he kissed her there as his hands made their way up the outside of her thighs. With one hand, he did undo the zipper and the dress fell away revealing mounds that were barely contained inside of black lace. He saw hard nipples waving at him. He felt obligated to introduce them to his mouth.

He covered one with his mouth, taking it in through the lace. When Danica's head fell back, he pulled the dress the rest of the way down her body, coaxing her to left up so that he could slide it out of the way. He didn't want any barrier between them that wasn't necessary for what they were about to do.

"Lovely," he said saucily.

Using only his tongue, he went in search of the flesh behind the lace.

Danica reached her hands to hold onto his head as Edrick allowed his tongue to touch every piece of exposed skin that he could reach.

"Sexy," he reverberated against her skin.

Reaching to each side of her, Edrick slid the thin material of her panties down her legs and off. When he inhaled her essence, Danica thought that she would orgasm right then and there. Seeing the satisfactory look on his face was compelling. When his finger slid between her legs and pressed against the soft folds of her womanhood, she felt her body lurch with a surprise yearning. Her hips moved along with the circular motion of his fingers. She was open and bare for his perusal.

Edrick needed more than a whiff and touch. Using

one hand, he encouraged Danica to lay back onto the bed. With her in the perfect position, he lifted her legs to rest on each of his shoulders as he kissed his way up her legs until he was able to give her the most intimate kiss possible. His plan was to get a taste and to test her readiness for him, but the moment his mouth came in contact with scent, he settled in for a feast.

"Sweet heaven," he declared.

Danica didn't have a chance to respond. Her head was spinning out of control. Edrick's tongue was loving her, his hands were on her ankles and her body shifted in sync with his mouth. She lifted her hips to give him better access when out of nowhere, lightning struck her core causing her to soar quicker than she ever had. Edrick's tongue was that magical. She was on a high that held her in its grip. This was pleasure beyond the meaning of the word.

Edrick didn't want to lose the momentum. He wanted to see Danica in this type of sexual haze for the rest of the night. Not wanting to give her a chance to come down from her release, he reached into the back pocket of his slacks and into his wallet. Taking out the condom, the likes of what he always kept there, he pulled out the gold packet and tore it open with his teeth. He had already replaced his tongue with his finger, not wanting to end her pleasure while he protected them from what was next.

He quickly divested himself of his slacks and briefs and stood to join their mouths in a searing mating that brought his hardness to an even stiffer, raging hardness.

When Danica opened her eyes and looked at him, his heart melted. He already knew that he wouldn't be able to be with her and walk away. He couldn't imagine not seeing her like this again and again.

Putting the condom in place, he moved quickly to join her on the bed, moving them together to the center.

"It's been a while for me," Danica admitted softly as Edrick slid between her legs as his tongue kissed a path across her neck.

"I'll go as slow as you want me to."

Danica breathed in deeply the minute she felt Edrick hard and straining as he slowly entered her body. She hadn't been able to get a good look at him, but from the way he had to work his hips to get himself planted inside of her, she knew his flesh was long and very thick. There was a little pain, but Edrick did her body good. He went slow as he said he would, allowing her body to adjust to his size. It wasn't easy, but it was pleasurable.

With him finally seated all the way inside of her, she grasped his shoulders and held on. When Edrick searched out her mouth, she gave into him willingly. His tongue mated with her in the same stimulating movements that his lower body was loving her. She could feel him everywhere.

"Baby!" Edrick declared.

Danica moaned louder, moving her hips in tandem with his. They were one as his thrusting increased. The wetness she knew he encountered made the act just as gratifying for her as for him. She grunted with awe, he growled with desire. Their bodies moved together as Edrick reached down to cup her buttocks, drawing her closer to his surges in and out of her body.

Danica kept with the rhythm even as Edrick increased the pace of his thrusts in and out with every stroke hitting her spot again and again. Her eyes watered and her body let go for a second time. Electricity sparked throughout her body as an intense fire invaded her womanhood, sending her flying higher and higher. Danica had to press her lips together to keep from screaming out her release like a wild banshee. It was surely how she was feeling.

Edrick wanted to prolong the feeling. He wanted to love her like this for hours and hours, but Danica's luscious body was singing a song and playing a tune that snared him. He felt his body rising and gripping him with a need to let his orgasm loose that he couldn't fight any longer.

Taking her mouth, hoping to suppress some part of the animalistic yelp he knew was coming from his belly, he kissed her and felt the vibrations of her moans, the screams she had been trying to keep in, but he knew the feeling was too great; he was engaged in the same plateau of desire that she was experiencing.

They climaxed together allowing their bodies to

claim each other. Edrick knew that his hips were surging into Danica. He would have pulled back some if she hadn't gripped his hips with her legs, holding him to her. They climbed together, crested as one and then slowed to a pace that kept the loving going, but with the feeling of accomplishment; both ways.

Edrick let his head fall against Danica's chest as he worked to control his rapid breathing. He could hear and feel Danica's breaths against the side of his face. She was struggling to gather herself just as he was.

"Am I still alive?" she asked, while caressing his bald head. Her body was doing its own brand of cheering after that race to pleasure. She needed that; she wanted that. She couldn't wait to have more.

"Whew! If you are, then I guess I am too."

Edrick continued to rock his hips into hers. Their loving wasn't over.

Danica rubbed his back, forming circles to drew attention away from how hard his was still breathing. He had put in work and he wasn't alone in that.

"That was amazing!" she declared.

"What was that you were doing with your hips. Damn, I have never!" Edrick declared, unable to find words to finish the statement.

"I don't know, but the night is still young. Can I do it again?" she asked, playfully.

Edrick leaned up and smiled at her.

"Yes, please and thank you very much!" he cheered.

7

It was morning; a good feeling kind of morning. The little bit of light that Danica could see through her barely opened eyes reminded her that it was the next day, Christmas Eve. Not only was that the case, but the weight of the arm that rested across her body recapped for her the events of the night before. She hadn't known what to expect when she entered Edrick's room once she made the decision that the only place she wanted to be was with him. Walking the short distance from the elevator to the door was an emotional one.

With her back to Edrick, who was still asleep and holding her close, she opened her eyes all the way and gazed out over the early morning bright sky. Through the opened blinds that led to the large balcony, she could see that several inches of additional snow had fallen since they arrived to his room. Everything about the early morning hour was quiet, serene and peaceful. For the first time in a very long time, Danica allowed her mind and spirit to rest; unlike the night before.

Heading to the room, her emotions tossed and turned in her head and in her heart. She knew what she wanted; she could sense what Edrick wanted. Why couldn't they just indulge? That questioned had actually plagued her all evening. They were consenting adults. Where she hadn't given the idea of being with him a second thought, digging into his life, the assignment in front of her was no longer clear. It wasn't until the door closed behind them and Edrick pulled her into his arms that she knew she wanted out of the task given to her. There was no way she could deny her attraction to him or the fact that he was more than words on paper and images on the computer screen. He was a man who, after one day, had already begun to mean more to her than any man she'd ever been with.

Moving slightly, Edrick's arm slid from its place around her waist to rest right on her hip. His grip was loose, but loving. His body warmed hers even as the flames from the electric fireplace kept the room nice and toasty. Waking before him was giving her a chance to think about her next move.

What she thought would be a night of just sex between them turned out to be so much more. The passion-filled intimacy delighted every part of her. Edrick's kisses stirred all of her senses. His touch had her believing that she was worthy of his attention and affection even though there was a sense of deceit on her part in the air.

After the catastrophe of five years ago, she hadn't

given much time to dating. Once a guy discovered who she was, all he wanted to talk about was how she made it through the scandal. Following that, his next move was to get her into bed thinking she was still as young and stupid as she had been with her affair with Jason. To stay away from all of that, she didn't do much dating. Instead, she focused on trying to get any part of her career started again. That brought about a sudden feeling of dread. Her mind started racing with a fear that he would wake up and have regrets about taking her to bed. She tossed between being afraid and being zealous with a powerful need for him. Her body purred with the thought that having two, maybe three hours of sleep, she found herself in the mood for more. Her desire for sex had never seemed so ravaging. The night had been filled with an unabashed ardent pull to teach other. After making love the first time, either he reached for her or she would reach for him; both ready to ravish each other.

At one point, Edrick had gotten out of bed and came back with a bowl of fresh fruit, sliced and looking amazing. To say they had worked up an appetite was an understatement. For hours, she was able to forget she wasn't a nice person. The guilt was growing.

Hearing Edrick moan in his sleep as he turned away from her reminded her that he didn't know who she was. He only knew the woman she chose to let him see; the one who needed to get close enough to him that she could get her job done.

Quickly, without warning, the bed felt cold. She shivered and pulled her arm around herself. She needed to breathe. She needed to think. She needed to talk to Hailey. She couldn't do it. She couldn't do what she was being asked to do. Edrick deserved better. She deserved a chance to have a job that wouldn't ask her to compromise who her heart told her she was. She didn't want to be the woman her bank account told her she needed to be if she were going to survive the industry. Money wasn't everything; not doing a wonderful man like this was.

She had the rest of the week in Denver and she wanted to spend it with Edrick, being who she truly was. She had to tell him the truth. Before that, she needed to release herself from the chains that had her bound. She needed to tell Hailey to pass the word to the powers that be that she was done. She was saying no to being used in such a way. She had no idea what that would mean for her career, but what she did know was that she could not face Edrick for another night like last night without him knowing the real, true Danica. It was Christmas Eve and she knew that there was no time like the present to clean up her life from a path that could hurt another person's life.

Years ago, she didn't care that Jason's life was ruined. When push came to shove, he had thrown her under the bus. He had the bigger platform. When the story broke, he claimed she had been aggressive in coming after him. That was far from the truth. She was still labeled as the woman who broke up a family and ruined a man's career. She did feel bad for Jason's wife and children. They had to endure the ridicule and scrutiny that came with what happened. She remembered that; her face being plastered everywhere, she couldn't forget it. She didn't want anything like that for Edrick. She'd fallen for him immediately. That was the wake-up call she needed as a reminder that there was still time to do the right thing. That is what mattered. She would then come back and tell Edrick everything. She could only hope that he would forgive her. If he didn't, she would understand. It would hurt, but she would walk away.

Closing her eyes, she wished really hard that if there was anything in the spirit of Christmas that could help her, she hoped some magic was in the wings to do just that.

Danica turned her head slightly and looked into Edrick's handsome face. Her eyes scanned his body down to where the comforter only came up to his waist. His muscled bare chest winked at her. There was a long, powerful part of him that moved slightly under the weight of the comforter. She remembered having him, all of him. Edrick had been tireless in his effort to please her. She'd never experienced such pleasure from a man. He loved hard, deep and with a purpose. From the moment his lean hard body had covered hers and loved her, the world fell away and she only felt. He gave to her, she gave to him and together they shuddered through eagerly awaiting release after release.

She kicked herself for being drawn into an uncompromising position hoped that once she revealed her truth, he would be as forgiving as the spirit of Christmas encouraged everyone to be. She needed that. She wanted that. She needed and wanted Edrick.

Moving as slowly and calmly as she could, she slid her naked body out of the bed. Her eyes scanned the room in search of her clothing. She needed to get back to her room. She had to make a bee-line for her phone, but not in Edrick's room. The conversation she needed to have with Hailey needed to be in a private place. She had a feeling shortly after, she would be jobless yet again, but this time, she didn't care. Perhaps, she wasn't cut out for the cutthroat business of journalism. It wasn't her if she was going to be tasked with tearing down someone's life in order to support the livelihood of others and herself. Since meeting Edrick, she now knew that making her own living wasn't worth the sacrifice of her own self-respect. She was worth more than what she has become.

Looking over to the bed, Edrick was still out, giving her a chance to slip away. She hated the reference to the walk of shame, but she was about to do that; that is, the act, not the feeling.

Searching around as quietly as she could, she looked for her shoes, finding them near the bedroom door. Her dress, she had walked right by it at the foot of the bed. Her thong and bra should have been easily noticeable, but she didn't see them anywhere. No way, could she turn on a light. The bright sky and the white snow should have illuminated the room enough to locate them. There was no way she could leave without them.

"You don't have to sneak out. If you're looking for those sexy panties, check under the comforter. I think I can feel something right under my foot."

Danica practically jumped out of her skin. Out of instinct knowing she was still naked, she pulled her dress around to cover the front of her body as she turned fully toward the bed and smiled.

"I thought you were asleep."

When Edrick winked at her from his place on the bed looking like a dream, she was tempted to go back and join him. Never had a man looked this good first thing in the morning. He was turned slightly on his right side with his head being held up by his right hand. The look on his face said he was enjoying watching her blush.

"I was until I realized I was alone in this bed. You're leaving? No goodbye or anything?" he asked jokingly.

"I'm sorry if that's wrong. I didn't want to wake you after..."

Danica didn't say the words. She was too busy remembering everything they'd done together. The many positions. The potent kissing. The seductive looks. The soft, tantalizing touches. Her body also remembered. It was willing her to drop her clothes and hop, not only back in bed, but on top of him. She couldn't. She had to clear her conscience prior to them having a repeat of the night before. If luck were on her side, after she came clean to him, he would still want her. She knew without any doubt that she wanted him, but not like this. Not as Danica Johnson. She needed to be Danica Green.

"What? After you zapped every bit of energy from my body last night and, well, early this morning, I was kind of hoping that I would be able to wake up to a little more before you had to leave for your spa appointment. That's this morning, right?" he asked.

Danica forgot all about that. Her only thought had been on reaching out to Hailey. She had an eleven o'clock appointment to get a massage, manicure and pedicure.

"Oh, yes, it is. I know that last night was sort of unexpected," she bashfully explained.

"But enjoyable, unexpected or not. I'm glad we did. Are you? In the light of day, are you good?" Edrick asked her.

Danica was better than good. So much so that she was close to revealing her truth to him right now. When the words were about to come out, she held back. She had to be able to come to him knowing nothing was being held over her head.

"I'm perfect," she boldly declared.

"Am I still going to see you later? I was hoping you could join me for lunch with Albert and Misha. They are anxious to meet the woman who had me out dancing last night."

The smile that crossed her face couldn't be denied.

"I would love to. You mentioned last night that you had a few work calls to make this morning. Why don't you do that. I'll call you when I leave the spa."

"Promise?" Edrick asked.

Danica walked over to the bed dropped her dress and shoes. Tre was something in his eyes and the way he asked that one word question that had her throwing caution to the wind. She decided to just go with what her heart and body screamed she wanted; Edrick. She wanted to show him how much she couldn't wait to see him later. Sliding the comforter from his body, she climbed back into bed, pulling it up over the two of them.

"Let me know if this is promise enough," she spoke sexily close to his lips before tasting them, going at them with the fervor of a starving woman.

In the next instant, she knew that the enthusiastic kiss on his lips was the start to the promise she was planning to keep. He groaned into her mouth as his hands slid down and around to grip her, pulling her right to the center of his body. Her little walk of shame and cleansing with Hailey could wait.

**

The moment Danica closed the door behind her, Edrick felt a sense of emptiness that he didn't expect. There was no doubt that the night before, they needed each other. There was something about the way they made love that felt like relief beyond the physical act. For him, it was like life had finally entered his body again. He'd been in a state of reserve to protect his heart for so long, that being with Danica was a breath of fresh air. He felt new; he felt more alive than he has in years. Being together was the exhale they needed. It was the sign that it was time to let go of what they hated about the Christmas holiday and instead, embrace the joy that others found in it year after year.

Moving away from the door, he went into the bathroom to check out the ridiculous grin he knew he'd find on his face. Danica was the reason behind it. He looked forward to seeing her later with plans to go skiing, something she had never done before. He looked forward to their date for him to teach her.

A date. That word was foreign to him, especially this time of year. His mind and heart were usually filled with anger and guilt. Should he experiencing more guilt for his desire to seek something fresh and new with Danica? She was still a woman he hardly knew, and now, he wanted to know everything. There was so much unbridled passion between them that he felt vulnerable; a feeling he hadn't experienced in a long time. He contributed that to feelings deeper than what was on the surface. He may have thought he wasn't ready for more with a woman, but Danica was already someone special. She was special enough that he was ready to do a formal introduction to his friends.

Speaking of them, he needed to make sure Albert and Misha were still planning to meet him for a late lunch.

Going back into the bedroom, he grabbed his phone and called Albert who answered on the first ring.

"Bro! I was looking for you at breakfast. Did you decide to eat in your room?" Albert asked.

Not wanting to share anything about his night before, Edrick changed the focus of the conversation.

"No. I slept in late. Listen, are you and Misha still free for a late lunch? Say, around three?"

"You know it. Even if we weren't, Misha was going to make it happen. She was mad that she didn't get the chance to really spend any time with you yesterday. She thought maybe you were going to get in your room and never come out. I told her you were at last night's concert. It was so crowded, she didn't see you after she made the introduction to the audience. She was both shocked and happy. You want to meet in the same restaurant? We have four of them here. Where you were last night is my favorite one."

"I loved the food. Everything was great. Look, I'm going to invite Danica, the woman from the plane. Remember her?"

"Ed, how could I forget. Besides, you mentioned in one of your texts that you were going with her to dinner and the concert last night. The way you were looking at her when you first arrived, I knew something was going on. I don't care if you just met her on the plane or not, this is all good stuff. That must have been a powerful conversation. Did the two of you have a good time at the concert?"

"Yes, we did. I had the best time. It's been a long time since I've enjoyed myself that much."

"That's only the beginning. Say, listen, how would you like to do me a favor? I don't want to put too much pressure on you. I had one of my Santa's come down with the flu. How would you like to get back into a Santa suit and wow the kiddies tomorrow morning?"

Edrick inhaled deeply. He hadn't done that since the year before Phaedra and Christian died. He was back at a place that held a lot of precious memories. Most of those were the light in the eyes of children when they saw him bounce into a room with a huge sack of toys over his shoulder. If he was getting back to life, that seemed like a plausible idea.

"I would love to. I'm here for the week. Whatever you need me to do, all you have to do is ask," he replied. The lack of hesitancy in his voice was a sure sign that he was ready to move forward and do so in many ways.

Albert chuckled in his ear as if he had just heard the best joke of his life.

"I'm going to hold you to that. I really need to meet this woman now. She really awakened something in you that needed to be woken up. I want to be able to tell her thank you. I feel like I'm getting my old friend back."

"You act as if we haven't been in contact with you in years. We talk at least once a week."

Edrick mentioned that just to be mentioning it. He knew what Albert meant. He was around, alive and kicking, but in a sense, he had checked out of all the things that had brought him joy in the past.

"You know what I mean. Anyway, we'll see you later. Misha can't wait to see you and to meet Danica."

"See you then."

Edrick walked over to the sliding glass doors that led to the balcony. He smiled seeing snow everywhere. His mood was festive. He was making a play for loving the Christmas holiday again. He had no doubt that flights would soon resume going out even with the new coat of snow. He would usually rush to get to a plane to get to Spain. This year, he was staying put. He was ready for all that the holiday would bring; especially more of the woman who was the cause of his smile.

8

Danica was frustrated after her fourth call to Hailey. She had left message after message to call her back and so far, she'd received nothing in response. An hour later and one hour before her spa appointment, she was still waiting. Any other time, Hailey would answer her phone on the first ring. Christmas Eve or not, she assumed her assistant would be working today. Danica was anxious as she paced around her room, hands wringing with worry. She needed to be done with the assignment. When her phone rang, she reached for it believing it would be Hailey finally calling her back.

"What took you so long? I've been calling you for almost an hour!" Danica shouted into the phone.

"You haven't been calling me? My phone hasn't rung all morning."

It wasn't Hailey. The unexpected voice on the other end was a pleasant surprise.

"Mason!"

It was her brother, her father's son but not her mother's. Her parents had split up over her father's affairs with other women many years ago. The only good thing that came out of that time was her brother, Mason.

"Hey, sis. I am missing you right now. I thought I was convincing enough that you would join us for Christmas. Pop said he asked you and you were thinking about it. I told him that your mom and your stepdad weren't going to be home to celebrate Christmas with you. Before you chastise me about the holiday, I know you don't usually celebrate it, but this is my last year at home. I'll be going off to college in the fall. I won't get to see you as much," he said.

Danica loved Mason and he loved her. They were years apart in age, but they were as close as siblings could be, even though they came from two different mothers.

"Fool, you will get to see me all the time. I plan to pull up on that campus anytime I want to. College costs a lot of money. I want to be sure you're not going to waste the money or the education. Sorry about Christmas, though. I told Pop that I got a last-minute assignment. You know I'm trying to fix my career. I do miss you."

"Can I come see you when you get back? I need some brother and sister time. Besides, what did you get me for Christmas? Pop said no to the PlayStation five, saying it costs too much. He wants me to pull my grades up."

"Are you trying?" she asked.

"Yeah, I am."

"I'll tell you what, I will get you one to keep at my place for when you visit. As soon as your grades are up, I'll let you take it home. I'll deal with Pop. That's the best I can do. And, I did get you a gift. I gave it to your mother who will give it to you Christmas morning."

"Where are you at on this assignment? Is it a good one?" Mason asked.

Danica never lied to Mason. She never wanted him to think that he couldn't trust her. He often confided in her. Even though he was only seventeen, he was often the person that kept her grounded along with her older brother who was more like a father than a brother.

"No, it's not a good one. I wish I had never said yes when I was asked."

"Why?"

"I thought this story would be the plateau to elevate my career. I made a big mistake and took it without thinking of the consequences."

"To you?"

"No, baby brother; to someone else. It's someone I'm finding myself wrapped up in on a personal level. If I go through with the assignment, I could hurt him."

There was silence after that. She walked around her room still wondering how to handle the outcome; how to deal with having the conversation with Edrick.

"Oh, you fell for someone? It's someone you're doing a story on?"

"I did and yes, it is. I didn't plan for it to happened. It just did."

"Then what's the issue? If this is going to hurt someone you care about, why would you agree to do it?"

"I didn't know that at the time. I was only thinking about my career and nothing else."

"Danni, you aren't getting into any trouble again, are you? The last time, I was young, but I remember how hard that time was for you. You don't hurt people and not suffer afterward. You tell me that all the time. You always tell me to treat people the way I want them to treat me. You say be nice and I will get nice back."

Smiling into the phone, she was glad her words were sinking in. It's too bad, she didn't often take her own advice.

"I know. I got caught up. I didn't look ahead or think about what could happen to this man's life. He's had something heartbreaking happen to him in the past. This story could bring all of that back to the surface for him. I'm sure he has worked hard to move beyond it."

"What are you going to do? Are you going to follow your heart or follow your dreams? See, I listen to you."

"Yes, you do. I'm going to follow my heart. I may need to find a new dream. This one isn't working out too good for me."

"What about your book? What happened to you writing a science fiction novel? You told me that you've always wanted to do that, since back in high school; maybe even before that. I think you could be a great author. Maybe doing things that could hurt someone isn't the ideal job for you; just a thought," Mason suggested.

Danica nodded even though he couldn't see her. Mason was definitely wise beyond his years.

"You'll be the first to know when I decide to write it."

"But you're still going to give up the assignment, right? I don't want you to get hurt, Danni."

"I love you, Mason. You have perfect timing with this call. You not only reminded me that I need to get back to loving Christmas because you will forever throw it at me for all the gifts Pop won't get you, but you remind me that Christmas is more than just a holiday. I forgot that. I do remember now. I promise you I'm going to back away from the assignment and go with my heart. I need to make a few phone calls. I won't be there tomorrow, but I promise I'll come by the week after the new year. We can hang out."

"Can you take me to look at cars? I can't get one until graduation and, again, only if my grades come up. I still want to look. If I go with Pop, he spends the whole time letting me look and ogle over cars to then shoot me down by saying I won't get it without better grades. I can do without the story time while shopping."

Danica laughed out loud. She knew how her father could be. She was around Mason's age when her father and mother split. She remembered how every time she asked for something in high school, it came with a speech.

"I got you. We can shop, without buying and without any speeches; I promise," she agreed.

"Keep your promise about the assignment too. Don't hurt anybody else, Danni."

The lump in her throat prevented her from responding right away. When her life fell apart, Mason, who was about twelve at the time, stood firmly in her corner. He didn't understand it all, but it didn't matter to him. What he knew was that his sister's face and name had been slandered on every television station and newspaper. People had called her horrible, disgraceful names. He had been hurt by it too. Whether she deserved that criticism or not, her family stood behind her, especially him.

"I promise you that the assignment is not going to be done by me. How's that?" she asked.

"That's perfect. Call me tomorrow to say Merry Christmas. You usually don't, but you seem to be in a better head space this year. Can I say that I'm loving it? I don't have to call you Scrooge anymore! I got that from your friends," Mason chimed.

Danica knew where he'd gotten it from. Her best friends, Toya and Kendra often parlayed every conversation around this time of year to calling her Scrooge. She spoke to them before her flight to Seattle and of course, they made that reference. She couldn't wait to introduce them to her Scrooge-less personality when she got back home.

"Nope, not anymore."

When her call with Mason ended, she tried reaching Hailey again. After two more tries and no pick-up, she resorted to the next best thing; an email. She grabbed her laptop and began typing so fast, her fingers were jittery.

From: Danica.Green@GBNNews.com

To: Hailey.Michaels@GBNNews.com

Subject: My Assignment – Edrick Stone

"Hi, Hailey. I've been calling you for the past hour. Why aren't you answering your phone? Anyway, I have some news, but it's not good news. I've had a change of heart. I've thought long and hard about this and I've decided that I'm not going to continue to try and get the story out of Edrick Stone. I don't feel right about this. I didn't when I got the assignment. I should have said something then, but I didn't. I think any attempt to do so without his full consent is an underhanded way to operate. I've done my share of being sneaky. I know everyone was counting on me. I'm sorry about that, but I can no longer live this lie in this way. When you get this email, please call me. I would like for you to relay to Mr. Gates and to Marilyn that there will be no story on Edrick. I plan to tell him of my deceit later today. He needs to know. I need to walk away from this. I'm sorry that my doing so will prevent anyone else from getting the story. I believe that if there is a story to be told, the focus of the story should do so knowing that it's being done. Edrick

or anyone else should be able to tell their side before anyone tries to air dirty laundry, whether there is any to find or not. I can't trick him into this. I need to be me. I will be around all day. Call me so that we can talk. If Mr. Gates would like to join the call, I'm okay with that too. I'm ready for whatever anger he will unleash. I will talk to you later. Merry Christmas from Danica Green, (not Danica Johnson)."

**

Edrick stood the moment Danica walked up to the table where he, Albert and Misha were sitting. Seeing her made his heart swell. Her strides toward him made him feel like a kid again.

After she left, he had gone to the resort store and purchased everything he would need for them to go skiing. He also bought extra clothes, jeans, sweaters and boots, which he had not packed because he was planning to be back home in Spain by now. Thankfully, Albert's stores were always equipped with anything and everything a guest would need. Being snowed in was always a possibility on the mountain. Being prepared for the needs of his guests was a priority. It was clear to him that Danica had also done a little shopping of her own. She walked toward him in jeans, a long, thick white wool sweater and winter green snow boots to match. The woman looked good in anything. He quietly acknowledged how he loved her naked the most. For now, he would keep that to himself.

"You made it," he said, pulling her into a hug.

Danica's bright eyes lit up in his direction and he was remembering the hooded gaze of her eyes as they made love throughout the night.

"I did," she said walking into his arms without hesitation.

Public displays of affection were not his usual reaction, but his mind had been on her since she left his room after rocking his world yet again. Before she had a chance to sit, he wanted to remedy his reception.

Moving back in her direction, he had a need, just a small one, of a sweet taste of her as his lips searched out hers. When her hand went to the side of his face as he kissed and stroked her lips with his, he didn't care who was around. He didn't allow his moment to be interrupted even when Albert cleared his throat reminding him of where they were.

"Leave them alone, Al," Misha declared.

"That's okay. He acts like my being happy irritates his demons," Edrick kidded.

"Whatever. Let the woman breathe," Albert replied jokingly.

"Danica, this is Misha, Albert's extremely beautiful better half. Albert, you met when you checked in."

Edrick waited until both Misha and Albert greeted Danica. When they were all seated and talking, nothing pleased him more than seeing Danica and Misha already bonding.

When Albert leaned toward him as the ladies chatted, Edrick didn't know what to expect.

"Look at my wife. She's so happy that you're happy. I'll assume we will have Danica to thank when this week is all over," Albert declared.

"Damn right. I'm thanking her right now in ways you have no idea."

The corner of Edrick's mouth turned into a smile when his eyes locked with Danica's. He winked; she winked in return and made his day.

"Spare me the details. I see it all over you in the light of day. Enjoy this time, my friend. The two of you hitting the slopes today?"

"We are. We're also gearing up for the game night tonight in the dining hall. She told me she's a pro at playing spades."

"Spades? You met a woman on a plane, connected with her immediately and she plays your favorite card game? Man, what did you ask Santa Claus for this year? Whatever it was, he is coming through. Or, maybe it was what Misha asked for. She's been dying for a moment just like this for you. It's been too long."

"I know it's been a long time since we've hung like this," Edrick said, agreeing with him.

"That's not what I meant. I should have said that it's been too long since I've seen the life return to your eyes. She would be happy you're finding the good in life again. Solitude is not the life Phaedra would have wanted for you."

Edrick nodded without replying. He didn't want to admit that he'd been thinking the same thing. He was happy that the Christmas week had just begun. He had something special planned for Danica on Christmas morning. With his suite having a full kitchen, since it was more like an apartment, he had ordered what he needed from the kitchen to cook her breakfast in the morning and hopefully, a very fabulous seafood dinner tomorrow night after he played Santa Claus. He was thinking about all the things he could do if he borrowed the Santa suit after using it. That's a thought, he said to himself. If Albert thought Misha was happy for him, he had no idea how happy he was for himself. Danica was the answer he didn't know there was a question out in the atmosphere for.

9

The hour was getting late and Edrick knew he was cutting it close to the time that he would need to pick Danica up at her room in order to spend the rest of the evening at the Christmas Eve game night. The resort had it all. Before jetting off to his own room to get dressed after he and Danica returned from skiing, he stopped by to see Horace in the restaurant who made sure he had what he needed to cook for Danica the next day. What he forgot to add to the list was a strawberry shortcake for dessert. Horace assured him that the remaining items on his list, including the festive decorations he asked for would be in his suite before he arrived back in it later that night.

Satisfied that he was all set, with an extra pep in his step, he turned to walk out of the restaurant and headed toward the elevator. Danica was expecting him within the hour.

"Edrick Stone?"

Hearing his name being called, he turned his head and cocked one of his eyebrows up in confusion. He knew the face from years ago, though he hadn't seen

Wade Douglass in years. The man, a powerhouse in the media industry, was now walking in his direction, making his way through the many festive red-cloth topped tables in the dining area that separated them.

"Wade?" he asked when the man reached him and held out his hand. Though it was barely visible under the thick black and gray down jacket, he shook the part of Wade's hand he could see.

"The one and only. I thought that was you I saw last night during the Mary J. Blige concert. Then, I second-guessed myself because you are usually secluded away from the public eye, not on the dance floor at a concert. How have you been?" Wade asked.

Edrick nodded at the realization that most people whom he encountered liked to make reference to how he enjoyed closing himself off to the world.

"I've been great; nothing to complain about."

"What a coincidence it is to run into you after years of trying to get an interview with you."

"Is that so? Wade, you know my story. I respect and appreciate every time your assistant and you have reached out over the year. I'm still not doing any interviews or stories. I enjoy my privacy. I know you can understand that."

"I hear you, old friend. I guess I'm just not beautiful enough for you to change your mind. I guess I lost out to the gorgeous woman you had in your arms last night. If I'm going to lose, I wouldn't mind doing so to a woman that lovely. I'm surprised you picked her to finally open up your life to. I see she's getting back in the game. Now, that was a shocker."

"I have no idea what you're talking about," Edrick frowned. He wondered what woman Wade could be talking about. The only woman he was with was Danica. Why would he make such a reference simply because he was out having dinner and dancing with her? He wondered why Wade needed to use such a cryptic message. What did he mean by saying she was getting back in the game?

The look on Wade's face was as confusing as he knew his own was.

"So, you weren't out having a nice evening after giving her an interview? I know that her paper is just as interested in your story as I am. You and I have history. I thought if you were going to finally open up after so many years out of the spotlight, that it would be with me. My paper has been good to you from the start of your career and through your way to the top, where you still reside. I finally stopped reaching out about a year ago when I came to terms that you were never going to give another interview to anyone. And then, I see you dancing and having a good time with the likes of a woman who had an earth-shattering calamity of a scandal associated with her name; I was shocked. Never in my wildest dreams would I picture she would be who you would grant your first interview to in, what, five years?" Wade asked.

The mention of five years sent a chill up Edrick's

spine. Still, he didn't know what Danica had to do with anything.

"Wade, if you don't stop talking in circles like all of you media people tend to do, I'm going to go insane with misunderstanding. Come out with it in plain English. Are you talking about Danica? The woman I had dinner with last night?" he asked.

"Of course. I saw you at dinner and I was going to approach you, but I assumed you were doing an interview over dinner. I saw her once reach to her purse under the table and it looked like she was operating a recorder or something. I caught that when you stepped away leaving her at the table alone. You weren't being interviewed? That is what she does. To see you back here on the mountain was enough of a shock. You know I still hurt for you over your loss. The two of you may have had a lot in common to talk about with what happened to you at the same time that she was going through her own, shall I say, heartbreak. I can't believe you didn't reach to me once you were ready to talk. I understand. My legs aren't as beautifully shaved as hers are," Wade joked.

Confused beyond any understanding, Edrick was trying to sort out the perplexing part of their conversation.

"Who are you talking about?" he asked Wade.

"Danica. Danica Green. Isn't that who you were with last night?"

"Oh, no. Her name is Danica, yes, but her last name

isn't Green, it's Johnson," Edrick explained.

He sighed with relief. He and Wade were not talking about the same woman. It's weird that the first names would be the same.

"No, I'm quite sure her name is Danica Green. She's one of the new investigative journalists for GBN News. They are ranked either number one or number two these days. My network is still trying to catch up with them."

This picture in his head wasn't right. He knew the news conglomerate, but Danica didn't work for them. She was in the medical profession. That's one of the first things she mentioned when they were on the plane.

"You must be mistaken. Her name is Danica Johnson. She not in news media; she's a nurse out of Seattle. You are really getting this mixed up. Is this your way of holding my attention long enough to get me to agree to a newsworthy segment with you about my life? I'm still not ready to do that. If I do, I'll let you know."

"You mean you haven't been working with her on a feature story? Perhaps you are and you don't know it. I promise you, I know who she is. You don't remember her, do you?" Wade asked.

Edrick moved them to the side so that they could have more privacy than standing out in the open. Dining guests were trying to make their way around the two of them blocking the way.

Something was wrong and he wanted to get to the bottom of it. It appears Wade had information that he didn't have. Danica wasn't Danica Johnson? Then who the hell was she, if Wade was right? He'd known Wade for most of his career. At one time, before he stopped granting interviews, Wade was his go-to person when he was ready to talk about anything that he thought was public-worthy. Wade was the journalist that he gave the exclusive interview to when Phaedra had given birth to their son. He had let the world into his private life. Wade and his team had handled it expertly. If he were ever planning to be front and center again, Wade is who he would call on.

"I need you to start at the beginning. I don't know what you're talking about. You're saying she's one person, yet she told me she was someone else," he explained.

Edrick was hungry for information. Had he been swindled into something? Had he been so caught up in her beauty that he'd let his guard down?

When Wade tapped his own temple on his head with his finger, Edrick knew he was about to hear a story.

"Look, you may not remember the story around her. I can tell you that right now, she's working for GBN News just as I told you. When I saw you with her last night, I was shocked. I called a friend at GBN late last night to find out what she was doing here with you. I admit, I was going to try and scoop you from them. I thought it looked like you were getting back out here. You were smiling and having a good time. When I saw you with her, I assumed it was for her to get a story on you. What I was told is that she was on an assignment for an undercover feature story, but my source there wouldn't tell me who. I didn't say that I had already seen her with you. That meant that you were her mark. She told you she was Danica Johnson? I don't know what name she's going by, but you need to check out Danica Green. I think at one time she may have been Danica King or something like that. The woman has many names, as some reporters do. She is talented, I will give her that. She snared the ever-elusive Edrick Stone."

"Really? What is it with the name Danica Green? What should I know?" Edrick asked.

If there was a story, he was well out of the loop. What as he missing? Why would she need so many names, if Wade was correct? His radar was being funky. There would be no reason for Wade to make any of this up.

"You really don't know? Okay, I think I know why you wouldn't know. There was a major story that was going on at the same time that you were going through your own family problems. Danica was mixed up with the boss at her old job. She was an up-and-coming journalist who had an affair with Jason Halston. Remember him? He lost half of his fortune when his wife found out about his affair with Danica. In fact,

Jason and Danica were on a plane to some romantic Christmas vacation when the story broke of their affair. He left his family behind, the wife and the kiddies, to frolic around with his mistress."

Edrick knew the name Jason Halston. What he didn't know was all the gossip behind how he lost his media empire. Edrick had been going through his own grief. That wasn't the time for him to be worried about someone else's. Still, this was intriguing. Who was Danica?

"You're sure the woman you saw me with last night is the same woman?" he asked.

"That I am. See, Jason didn't know that his wife had hired a private investigator to get the dirt on him. Man, it was dirty. Jason tried to save face by saying Danica used him to ride to the top in a play for the anchor desk. With his money and power, he dragged her like no woman has ever been dragged. There were memes about her, trashy stories about their hookups and photos. The photos were of the two of them on islands, heading into hotels and much more. They labeled her as the ultimate goal-driven, gold digging, goal-digger. It was brutal. It took a few years for that light on her life to dim. It appears she has resurfaced. Her secret assignment must be to get close to you to get a story. Look, there are a lot of us who want to get an exclusive with you. I'm not telling you this to get that story from her to me. It looks to me that you didn't know any of this was going on. I bet Miss Danica is back and up to her old schemes."

Edrick didn't know if he should believe Wade or not. Why would the man lie to him? Yes, he wanted a story; him along with dozens of other journalists had been trying to get the story behind his steady rise to fame, but he wasn't talking. Many wanted to know how he was able to stay on top and not crash and burn when his family was taken away from him.

"You're sure this Danica you're speaking of is the one I was with?" he asked.

"Yeah. I saw you with her, Albert and Misha earlier today, as well. I'm telling you, that's Danica Green. Now, this morning, I made another call to another connection I have at GBN and she gave me more information about her. I was hoping to have a chance to talk with you. Her getting a story, I'm good with that. Her trying to swindle you, that wasn't going to fly. I would say this is fact, but you know, a source is a source until they aren't. I can only tell you what I was told."

"I hear you," Edrick accepted. He only wanted to hear all that Wade knew.

"She was, allegedly, sent on an assignment to try to discover if there was a chance that you got rich and continue to maintain it by running some kind of Ponzi scheme, the likes of Bernie Madoff. Remember him? He died in jail after being charged and convicted of being the mastermind behind the nation's biggest investment fraud. The likes of what he did ended up costing investors millions of dollars. I'm telling you, who you were with last night is the same woman I'm speaking of."

Edrick waited while Wade pulled his phone from his pocket and scrolled through it.

"Ponzi scheme? That again? How many times is anyone going to keep looking only to find it's not true? The IRS and every other federal organization have looked into me and they never found anything," Edrick explained. He was saying the words more for himself than for Wade.

"Like I said, the journalist in me never sleeps. Even though I'm on vacation here with my wife for Christmas, I promised her another trip for Valentine's Day if she let me get in a little work."

Edrick tried to look at the screen on Wade's phone.

"What did you find out?" he asked.

He really was curious now. If Danica wasn't who she professed to be, that would mean that everything they shared, including the night before, was a part of her lie; an even bigger scheme than a Ponzi scheme.

"From the notes I took from my call, my source at GBN stated that they wanted to do a story on your life since your wife and son died. They wanted to know what you've been up to. You own quite a few brokerage houses and all are doing better than any others, even those on Wall Street. Though all appear to be legit, GBN wanted to know if there was something going on that getting closer to you would reveal. That was Danica's job. My source's exact words were that his boss, Warren Gates, tasked Danica with finding out how a black man with your wealth from trading and investing, etc., was maintaining such wealth without being a public figure over the past five years. He believes there's a story and he tasked Danica with exposing you by any means necessary. He said he knew because he was in one of the meetings before she was whisked off to Seattle to meet your plane. It was all a setup. I wasn't too sure until you told me that her name was Danica. There is no way two women have the same name, considering how rare it its. I'm sorry to lay this on you like this. I would love the story, but not like this. I have enough respect for you to not let you go down like this. I saw you earlier right here in the restaurant. You looked like you were smitten with her. I'll just say this and I mean no disrespect, but Jason was too. Look what happened to him. You need to pull out your phone or tablet and look into who Danica Green is. She's not Danica Johnson, some nurse from Seattle. She's lying to you."

Edrick was on fire and not in a good way. When Wade clicked a few buttons on his phone and turned it around so that he could see, Edrick looked into the eyes of the woman who'd made love to him all night long. They were the eyes of a woman he thought was as open and honest as he was being. Clearly, he was mistaken when he looked down below the photo. Her name was what Wade said it was. Back then, she'd been Danica King, but she was now going by Danica Green – not

Danica Johnson.

Snatching Wade's phone more aggressively than he had planned, Edrick scrolled and scanned an article dated the same week that Phaedra and Christian had died. He couldn't believe what he was reading.

"What the hell?" Edrick shouted. He continued to scroll as he read more and more.

"Hold up. I want you to see one other thing. Here is an email from my source. It's the one from six months ago when Danica was hired, welcoming her to the company. He was able to pull it and share it with me."

Edrick waited patiently. The minute Wade handed the phone back to him, he knew he'd been had. He now knew that Danica had been running a game on him. Was she that cruel that she took it far enough to sleep with him to get close enough to him? Perhaps, she was trying to find a way to get access to files and emails. Whatever the game was, it was over now. He needed to talk to her.

"Can you send me that email? Maybe not the part that shows who sent it. I just need the body of the email that has her picture and the announcement of her joining GBN News."

As Wade punched in characters to send him the email, Edrick could barely remain standing in place. He needed space. He appreciated getting the heads-up from Wade, but he needed to get some air. He needed a place to clear his head before he approached Danica with what he knew. He hoped she had a good story for what she was doing to him. Just when he thought the holiday would have new meaning, his world tanked again. He'd fallen for a woman who manipulated him with her brains, her beauty and her body. He'd fallen for it with everything in him.

No longer interested in talking, he thanked Wade and walked off. Yes, he'd heard enough. Now, he needed to hear from Danica. As he walked with strong, purposeful strides, he remembered why he lived a life on the outside of people. They couldn't be trusted. He wondered what kind of woman would set out to get a story and do the things they did the night before. He felt her giving herself to him completely. Could she be that cunning that he couldn't tell he was being played? He would soon find out.

10

Danica walked up to what she believed was Albert's personal office at the resort. After changing her clothes after the ups and downs on the ski slopes, literally and figuratively, she was excited that tonight, she was going to tell Edrick everything.

After finally talking to Hailey who had fired off a heated email back to her from Warren, she held her ground that she would come clean with Edrick, exposing all of them and what they were planning to do. Unlike the team at work who could walk away with life as usual claiming they were doing what occurs every day in the life of a news media empire, she, on the other end, didn't know what Edrick's reaction would be. They had spent an amazing night together. That was followed up with him being patient with her as a first-time skier. She did pretty good considering she spent most of the time on her behind. In the end, it was all in fun and well worth it. She hadn't had this much fun in years. Earlier had not been the right time, but tonight was the time to finally come clean. She knew it was the right thing to do.

She had been waiting on Edrick to come by her room to scoop her up to spend Christmas Eve together when he sent her a text asking her to meet him at Albert's office. She noted the directions to where it was. She thought it odd, but let it go. Her only thought was that she was going to be able to spend the rest of her time at the resort with Edrick with everything behind her except for what could be possible with him. She was believing that telling him everything would sting at first, but knowing how she felt about him is what she hoped would soften the blow.

Standing outside of Albert's office door, she took a long breath, checked her outfit, a beautiful Christmas sweater, since an ugly sweater contest would also be happening tonight, another pair of jeans and a pair of low-heeled boots. She had pulled her long hair up into a tight bun on top of her head and decided against any makeup. Tonight, she wanted to be free; she wanted to be Danica Green.

Knocking lightly on the door, she was surprised when it opened and Albert was on the other side, letting her in. She assumed he and Edrick must have had some kind of meeting, which is why she was meeting him here instead of at her room. She knew that they had talked business a little earlier in the day.

Walking inside, seeing only a half-smile on Albert's face, she was surprised to find Edrick with his back to her as he focused on something outside of the large three-paned glass windows that made up an entire wall in the office.

"Hi, Danica. I'm going to leave you and Edrick to talk," Albert said.

Danica felt a major frost in the air. The heat was on but the vibe she got from Albert was arctic cold. The fact that Edrick still had not turned around astounded her. All day, he'd been happy every time he saw her. She enjoyed a day of spontaneous kisses whenever the mood struck either one of them. She wondered what was wrong. She was about to walk over to him when Edrick turned in her direction.

"Albert, stay, please," Edrick said, speaking in a harsh, almost brazen tone.

Danica looked between the two men and didn't like the vibe. The door to the office was still open. In fact, Albert had opened it all the way and left it that way. As cozy as the space appeared to be in decorations in warm hues of various shades of blue, she was still surprised at the coldest treatment.

"Is something wrong?" she finally asked.

Neither man would look directly at her. They only looked at each other. When Edrick finally turned to her, she took a step back. Gone was the soft, intoxicating amatory gaze she often found in Edrick's eyes. That look was replaced by one of steely, uncaring, almost disgust. What was happening? She looked to Albert for help. Instead, what she got was him walking toward the window, keeping his back to them. It was clear Edrick wanted to talk to her, but he didn't want to do it alone.

"Danica, I have something unsettling I want to talk to you about. I didn't want to do it in a room with us alone, which is why Albert is here," he explained.

With no sense of warmth from him, she needed to know what was going on.

"Edrick, you're scaring me. What's wrong?" she asked again.

"Your name. Your name is wrong. What's your name?" he asked.

She tilted her head and gazed up at him more intently this time. What was he talking about? Her name?

"I don't understand. My name? My name is Danica. You know that," she explained.

"I know your first name is Danica. What's your full name; first and last?"

Edrick put both of his hands in his pocket as he leaned back against the glass top desk in the center of the room. When he crossed his legs at the ankles and looked at her sternly, the look in his eyes told her that he knew. How much, she didn't know, but he knew her last name wasn't Johnson. That had to be why he was asking.

She started to keep up the farce until they could be alone, but she knew there was no need. This was a moment she didn't want to have. She wanted to be able to control the narrative of how he would find out about her true intensions. She wanted to be able to explain before he found out about her assignment.

"Merry Christmas Eve!"

Everyone turned to a voice from the hall outside of Albert's office. Danica didn't see who it was as the person kept walking. No one smiled or acknowledged the holiday greeting. There was no celebratory mood in the room.

Knowing she had to do it now and feeling deflated, she felt her body let go of the tension that flowed through it. She closed her eyes, lowered her head and let her arms drop down against her sides. This was it. There was no turning back.

"Danica Green. It's not Danica Johnson," she uttered lowly and with great sadness.

She heard Edrick's loud exhale of air from his lungs. His gaze turned colder, if that were possible. There was no feeling for her in his face. There was nothing that looked like that man whose face, just the night before, showed so much compassion and passion that she was overwhelmed with loving feelings for him. Falling for him came out of nowhere and fast. She had a hard time keeping up with the intense feelings that had been growing by the minute. She was now face-to-face with her deceit. She had no resolve other than to put it all out there.

"Why were you on the plane out of Seattle? You're not a traveling nurse or anything close to the nursing field. You don't even live in Seattle. I know, but I want you to tell me. I need to hear you say it," Edrick remarked.

"Edrick, I swear I was going to tell you tonight. I really was. I was waiting for the right time. You were going to pick me up in my room and I was going to tell you. I prayed that once I did, you would find it in your heart to forgive me. I know it was wrong. I knew it all along. I got caught up in who you are; the man I met on the plane. I am so sorry. I hope you will let me explain," she pleaded.

Danica could feel tears welling up in her eyes. She was breathing hard. Her foot began to tap uncontrollably. That happened whenever she was nervous. She'd never been more scared in her life. She wasn't scared of Edrick or Albert. She was afraid that what she hoped was a beginning was actually an ending to something beautiful between them. Looking at Edrick, there was nothing in his gaze that said she would leave the office hopeful.

"Why were you on the plane?" he asked again.

"I was on assignment for GBN News. I'm an investigative journalist for the network. I'm assuming you already know that."

"I do. I also know why you were there. I know who you are. I just needed to have you say it," he said.

Before she could again apologize, Edrick took his hand from his pants pocket and reached for a stack of papers behind him. Pulling only one around to hand to her, Danica gasped in despair. In the center of the paper in her hand was her photo surrounded by the story of what happened between her and Jason. She didn't need to read the entire article to know what it said. She had lived it. She was there. Edrick knew her secret. When he said he knew who she was, he meant it. His knowledge went beyond what she initially thought.

"Edrick..."

"Why would you set me up like this? Is this just something you do?" he asked.

Danica was about to reply and then Edrick handed her even more papers, including one that was the announcement of her employment with GBN. That was an internal email. She wondered how he got it. It really didn't matter; he had it.

"Oh, my goodness. I really can explain this," she said, rushing the words out.

"Can you? You mean you can explain to me your past and how it's not relevant right now? Can you explain how you opened up your mouth and lied to me about who you are? You have something valid that would delight me about how you were planning to dig for dirt on my life? You came into this thinking I was some kind of crook, some thief? You thought I was stealing money from clients? What, you didn't think I was the kind of man who could go out and secure my wealth the legal way? Before you try to counter any of that, I made a lot of phone calls over the past hour. What I was able to find out about why you're here has

144

been revealing. In fact, so much was revealed that it's hard to think you're the same woman who spent the night with me last night," he said sadly.

Danica was surprised at the calmness to every word he spoke. She knew he was angry. At this point, with him knowing everything, she thought that he would be flying off the handle. That's the reaction she would get from most men when she had bad encounters with them. This Edrick before her was hurt; he was crushed. He was containing his anger, but she could feel it in the air. She could read it in his eyes. She saw eyes that didn't brighten and shine at the sight of her. She wanted the warmth in his eyes to return. This is what she didn't want to happen.

"I'm sorry. I'm so sorry. It started out as an assignment; you started out as an assignment. Then I got to know you and that changed. Everything changed," she explained.

"When? This morning? Just now? Last night? Was last night a part of the plan?"

"No! Last night was real; that was all real. I was going to tell you the *truth*!"

Danica shouted that one word so loud that Albert turned around and faced them. Edrick stood straight up after hearing her declaration.

"We slept together last night and this morning. You had a lot of chances to tell me the truth. I had to hear it from someone else who recognized you. I had to spend my time today checking into you in a way I never thought I would have to. You lied to me. You slept with me and still, not a single word all day. How could you do this? Before you answer, let me explain something to you. I made my money the honest way like the majority of others in my field. I've been the best at numbers since elementary school. People were telling me back then that I had a mind like a calculator. I turned my knack for numbers into a career. I was taught by the best. He taught me to do things the right way. I've had a lot of ups and downs in my life. I lost my wife and son in a tragic way. Were you hoping to get more information on that as well? I told you the most intimate details of losing them. You know what that did to me and my life. Did you have some kind of recorder with you last night while we were at dinner together? Did you do that?"

Stunned that he would know that, she didn't know how to answer that.

"I..I.."

"Don't bother. A friend saw you with it when I stepped away from the table during dinner. You never know who knows who."

"I'm sorry."

"Save it. Going back to my work, my business thrived because I have the best team in the world. They also know that I would be the first to report any of them if I thought they were doing something illegal. You let some guy use you to push his own career to the top. You let him set you up on a mission to find something to tear me down. I wouldn't be the first man you tore down, now would I?" he asked facetiously.

Danica heard his disgust for her in his voice. She was ashamed. The last revelation stung. The words cut into her life a sharp knife. There is no doubt he was talking about Jason and what happened. She had the article in her hand along with a dozen others. She knew what was in them. She still kept copies at home as a reminder of what not to do for any reason. She failed to check herself when she decided her job was more important than a man's personal world. Even if she had come up with nothing, her boss would probably twist what she would have found out and turned it around to hurt him. How could she be here again? How could she justify to herself the fact that she was once again hurting another man?

"Edrick, please let me try and explain myself. I have so much to tell you about what's been on my mind yesterday and today. It's not only what you've discovered."

She wanted to continue, but Edrick held his hand up to stop her. It was clear to her that he'd heard enough already.

"Danica, I can't do this. Do you admit that you sought me out to gather information for some kind of exposé on me? You made love to me like a woman who desired me as much as I desired her. You know my vulnerabilities. You knew what this holiday meant to me. I thought I had found a new reason, a new purpose to love the holiday. My goodness, being around you was a breath of fresh air. Now I find it was all a ploy. Was sleeping with me a ploy too? I can't talk to you about this anymore right now. I know all I need to know. Trust me, that was too much."

"Edrick, please," she pleaded.

He moved to go around her. Without warning, she cried. It wasn't just him not wanting to talk or even look at her. It was because once again, she chose the wrong path. A man she cared more about in two days than she has for any man she's ever been involved with can't stand the sight of her.

"You should have told me. No matter what else you have to say, by now, you should have told me. You didn't and I don't believe that you were. I assume that's just another lie. Al, thanks for letting me use your office. I'm out."

"Ed, the kids tomorrow?" Albert asked.

"I'll be there. They deserve that. *No* one else deserves anything from me; not even my time."

"Let me explain!" Danica yelled at Edrick as he walked away.

He was gone before she entered the outer office. With tears streaming down her face, she turned back to Albert.

"I didn't mean to hurt him," she said.

"But you did. That being your intension or not, you did. He has been through hell and back. Him coming back to the guy you got to know for the past two days has been dormant for five years. He could not get over the grief being able to save Phaedra and Christian, his family. He was falling for you. He was actually afraid of how powerful his feelings were becoming for you after just two days. We were talking about that this morning. Do you know what I said? I told him to go for it and not hold back. He came back from a dark place all from a plane ride and talking to an amazing woman. Who are you? Why did you have to be someone other than who he met?"

"He did meet me. I swear I was going to tell him."

"Before or after you dug up dirt on him? He's been through enough. There is no dirt. He is as honest as they come. He has helped thousands of people see their dreams of wealth when they had no clue about the stock market or even saving. Hell, I have my resorts because I listened to him. He never steered me wrong. He is and has always been hands on because he cares. He cares deeply. His moving in a direction toward you, the first woman since his wife that he even thought to mention to me? That took a lot for him to do. It wasn't even that you were here. It was that he felt a strong connection to you. It was something he wanted to explore for the first time in years. Now he finds it was all a mockery; a charade. I need to go check on him. I would advise you that if you planned to reach out to him, give him some space. I need to go make sure my friend doesn't go back into his shell. The worse part of all of this, is that it's occurring over Christmas; that was when he lost his family. Now this."

After Albert left her standing alone, Danica covered her cries with her hand and raced to find a bathroom. Knowing she had passed one on her way in, she ran to it, went inside one of the stalls and cried until her chest hurt. She didn't care anything about herself or the threats she'd received from Warren on the call she'd taken from him just before she left to meet Edrick. He could have her job. She didn't care. She only cared that she had hurt Edrick. She saw it in his eyes. It was a ghastly look that she never wanted to see coming in her direction ever again.

She had a feeling this was unfixable. There was no way she could remain at the resort. Gathering herself, she looked for a way to get to her room without taking the elevator. She didn't want to see anyone. Going from one hall to the next and then to another, she found an exit sign for the stairwell that led to the corridor where her room was. She needed to get a plane out of Denver. She couldn't face Edrick after what she did. It was time for her to go home and face another Christmas that turned tragic because she screwed up.

11

Christmas Day

The early morning knock on her hotel room door on Christmas morning was one Danica had been waiting for. She had called down to the front desk and asked if someone could assist with her luggage. Though she arrived with only two pieces, she had to buy an extra piece from the resort store because of the extra clothes she'd bought the day before. With a flight out later in the evening to take her back to Chicago, she figured she would get a head start and get to the airport early. Leaving was not her preference, but after her encounter with Edrick, what else could she do. The hurt in his eyes did her in. She had to leave.

Danica let her eyes scan the room, making sure she wasn't leaving anything as she made her way to the door. The night before had been grueling. She missed Edrick. She thought about what he must have been going through. The painful hurt look on his face haunted her for the rest of the evening. She tried to get a flight out the evening before, but the airlines were all booked now that flights had started taking off and landing again. She was hoping to get on one, but the next available flight wasn't until nine in the evening. It was only ten in the morning and it was Christmas Day. She didn't mind sitting in the airport for most of the day.

After returning to her room to tons of texts, calls and emails from the office, she ignored them all. The last that she had listened to was from Warren telling her that she had better keep her mouth shut and do her job or she need not come back to work; *ever*. She chose the latter. She didn't have any fight left in her. She'd even read an email from Hailey who told her that she was ruining everything for both of them. Both of them? She wondered what Hailey thought her own stake in all of this would be. She was an assistant.

In the middle of the night, after every attempt to get any sleep failed, she typed out her resignation and sent it before she was finally able to get a few hours of sleep after letting go of the weight of the job. It was too much. She left her phone off hoping to avoid any contact. She was startled when another knock on the door, faster and harder this time, reminded her what she was supposed to be doing besides thinking about the day before. She hurried to open the door. Standing on the other side wasn't a hotel employee coming to take her bags downstairs, but instead, there was Misha with fire in her eyes. The look on her face matched the one on Edrick's face the day before.

"How could you?" Misha yelled from the hallway.

Danica was startled by the sheer anger directed at her, though she understood it. Misha cared for Edrick like a brother. The day before, they had enjoyed their late lunch and the chance to get to know each other. Right now, that didn't matter. What did matter was Misha was upset that her friend had been hurt. Danica was ready to face the firing squad.

"Misha, I'm sorry. Please come in. I can explain. Edrick wouldn't let me explain my truth to him."

She moved to the side to let Misha inside of the room.

"You're leaving?" Misha asked, seeing the luggage near the door.

"Yes. I thought you were someone coming to get them. I was able to get a flight out and back home tonight. I know Edrick doesn't want to run into me while he's here. He is still here, right?" she asked.

"Yes, he is. I'm not letting him leave. He was considering it last night. I threatened bodily harm if he tried to leave this mountain in the state that he's in. If he did, it may be another year before Al and I see him again. That's unacceptable. How could you do that to him? How? I don't understand how you could portray to be someone who cared about him. You were living a lie to get close to him; to expose something that wasn't there. That's a terrible thing to do to anyone and Edrick cared about you. I don't even think he fell for Phaedra that fast. You want to explain something, I'm all ears. Let's hear it. What do you have to say for yourself?"

Misha asked.

"Please, have a seat."

Danica motioned for a space on the sofa where she joined her.

"No lies," Misha warned.

"No more lies. First, let me say that I truly am sorry for what I did. I don't really have an excuse for doing what I did other than to say it was a part of the job. I was doing what any other reporter or journalist would do."

"Including sleeping with him? Yes, Al told me about that. What kind of woman are you?"

"No, not that. I did that because I fell hard for Edrick. Outside of the assignment I was on, I really did fall for him; pretty much instantly. On that plane after talking for two and a half hours, there was no way any woman wouldn't be attracted to all of him. Then we got here and all we did was have fun, something I haven't done in a long time. We talked and shared. It felt natural and right being with him. Yes, I slept with him. It was the best night of my life. I didn't have a care in the world. He treated me like a porcelain doll, with so much care. It wasn't just the sex, but it was everything about being with him. I have never been a believer in love at first sight, but I'm telling you, that's what happened. Putting aside my past and what I've done, again, not making excuses for that either, this was different. I'm assuming you know about that too?"

Believing that Misha would have gotten the entire

story before approaching her, she was hoping she wouldn't have to go into too much detail about how she ended up on her assignment.

"Yes, my husband gave me the rundown on your past. We were up most of the night worry about Ed. How could you do this if you claim to care about him so much? Make it all make sense to me," Misha exclaimed loudly.

Danica had to get this out. Edrick didn't let her but she was hoping that in the end, Misha would be an advocate for her with him. She needed him to know that she was going to come clean.

"Yes, I set out on an assignment in the very beginning. The minute I sat next to him on the plane and he smiled at me, I was already hooked. We talked so easily with each other. It was as if we were meant to meet and have the amazing connection that we did. I would say that once I left that airport, I never thought about the real reason I was on that plane."

"Ed said something about a recorder while at dinner? How could it be that you weren't thinking about it anymore, yet you were recording your conversation?"

"There's nothing on it. I did remember I had it, but it wasn't recording. I even checked it to be sure it was off. For a second while in my room, I thought I would get proof that Edrick was a good guy. I wanted to convince my boss that the assignment was for naught. At dinner, I realized I didn't even want to do that. I didn't record anything," she admitted."

She watched the tension leave Misha's body as she sagged back against the chair.

"Okay, I believe you. I feel like I should be angry with you forever because I will always be team Ed. I can see in your eyes that you're being sincere. What about the assignment?"

"It no longer mattered. I didn't get a chance to tell Edrick that. He walked out on me in the midst of his anger. Two days ago, I had already decided I wasn't going to do the job. I only wanted Edrick. I knew what I was going to tell my boss, but I didn't get around to sending the message until yesterday, early in the morning after I left his room. I promise you with everything that is in me that the idea to tell Edrick the truth came up way before we slept together. I wanted that because I wanted him. I tried reaching my assistant for a few hours. She wouldn't reach back to me. When she finally did, along with my boss on the phone, I told them I wasn't doing the job. I hadn't given them anything nor was I going to. Yes, Edrick shared a lot with me since we met. He told me about his work. He also told me about his wife and son. He's a loyal, caring and compassionate man that any woman would be lucky to have in her life. I needed a little time to tell him what I had been doing and why. I wanted to do it in a way that I hoped he would believe me and not hate me. I'm in love with him; I am in love with Edrick. It's not about money or status or anything. It's about the magnificent man I encountered on the plane. He was the man who thought it not robbery to pay for everyone on the plane to be put up at your wonderful resort in any accommodation they chose. I learned immediately that everything he does, it's from his heart; it's from a good place. He told me about his friendship with you and Albert and how that began. He talked about how they lived out the dreams that started on a college campus. He shared a lot with me. Not one word of that would I ever repeat to anyone other than you. I was going to tell him. I wanted to make sure my job knew they had nothing coming."

"Did you actually do that?"

"I did. Even under the threat of breach of contract, yes, I did. They can sue me for not doing the job they paid me to do, but I don't care about that at all. I care about Edrick and what he's going through. I promise you, I was going to tell him. I even have proof."

Danica remembered her email to Hailey and the subsequent exchange with Warren that turned nasty with his yelling, screaming and vital threats. When she thought about Edrick, it all rolled off of her shoulders. She welcomed their punishment, even if it meant her no longer having a job. She's been there before. This time, she would be able to control the narrative of what her actions brought about.

"What proof? Proof of what?"

Feeling a rush of excitement, Danica raced to her bag and found her laptop. Signing onto it, she pulled up the email exchanges. She specifically pointed out her first email to Hailey early that morning after leaving Edrick's room telling her that she was no longer doing the assignment. She pointed out the time of the email exchange to Misha. She remained quiet while Misha read it all.

A few minutes later, their eyes connected.

"You're telling the truth."

"Yes, I am. I wanted to tell that to Edrick, but he was too angry to look at me anymore. I don't blame him. I do love him and I didn't mean to hurt him. I got caught up in doing a job I have no business doing. I'm not cut out for this cutthroat kind of work of digging into people's lives without them offering up the information willingly. In the end, I quit."

That word got a rise out of Misha. Danica didn't feel any better about what she had done to Edrick, but it gave her some relief knowing that she had put a stop to GBN's plan. This way, they wouldn't be able to send anyone else. She was also silently happy that she had been the one they sent. If Edrick never talks to her again, he gave her the most magical few days of her life. She would never forget that or him.

"You quit? You actually quit your job?" Misha asked.

Danica nodded. She was happy that she had the balls to do it.

"You didn't show any of these emails to Edrick? He should read these. He should know that before he approached you with what he knew, you were already planning to tell him the truth. He needs to know that you fell in love with him. I looked in your eyes when you were saying everything and I believe you. I'm not an easy cookie to win over, especially when it comes to him. He's the brother I never had. If I had a brother, I would want him to be exactly who Edrick is. I think he loves you too, but he hasn't said so. That's why he was so hurt. He fell hard and fast; that has never, ever happened to him before. Sure, he's been in love, but there is something different when he speaks of you; something I've never seen in his eyes before."

Danica shook her head, lowered it and then looked back up right at Misha.

"Not even..."

Misha cut her off.

"No, not even with her. They had been going out for months and it was pretty casual. About six months in, he told Albert he was falling for her. I had just started dating Albert around that same time. When I saw him looking at you and what I saw, that was new. Albert said the same thing when he saw you checking in. He told me that he needed me to meet you because there was a light in Edrick that he hadn't seen in a lot of years. He had a feeling it had to do with you. I had the chance to talk to Edrick last night when he thought he was going to leave here early. I think he was going to stay through tonight and leave tomorrow morning. I threatened him if he tried leaving here before his seven days with us were up. He knows I mean it," Misha jested.

Danica finally felt a reason to smile when Misha laughed.

"I don't know what to do. I don't want to leave here and not see him again. I didn't know what else to do. If my presence causes him more pain, I would gladly leave to give him some peace. I know what the holiday has done to him. I don't want to add to that. He's been happy."

"A lot of that has to do with you."

"I've been so stupid; again."

"We all make mistakes for whatever reason. At least I know you were trying to make it right. I know how you feel about him and that matters."

Danica was close to crying. She needed someone in her corner. She was glad it was Misha.

"Thank you," she said.

Danica didn't know what to think when Misha stood suddenly and handed her back the laptop. When she walked toward the door, Danica nervously followed her. At the door, Misha turned to her with a straight face, one filled with warning.

"I'm going to tell you like I told him, if you try to leave this resort, I will hurt you."

Danica waited for a smile on Misha's face to follow the threat, but none came. The woman was serious. Danica believed her.

Danica laughed out loud. She knew Misha was

joking while at the same time, very much serious.

"Hilarious," Danica kidded.

"Look, I am not going to lose being in contact with Edrick again. I also think that what you've done is worth forgiving. I want to see him happy. I want that my any means necessary. He's spent a lot of years existing, but not living. Sure, work for him continues to prosper, but I need him to get back to living a life work living beyond work. His heart is hurting and his ego probably took a hit, but that's not enough to walk away from what I think the two of you could have together. Yeah, it's been two days but I know couples who have spent a lifetime together after only a few hours of meeting. Al and I have seen that plenty of times right here at our resort. It happens and yes, I believe it has happened to you. Maybe it's the Christmas spirit or something, but it's in the air. Don't leave. Please stay."

"You mean that?" Danica asked, hopeful. She wanted nothing more than to have Edrick's forgiveness.

"Absolutely I do. Edrick is playing Santa about right now. I think you should come and join me. Perhaps you can tell Santa what you want for Christmas. Don't leave here if he hasn't said he doesn't want to see you anymore. If there is a chance, fight for it. If you walk away, neither of you will win. What do you say you leave this luggage here and let's go have a festive day? I like you. Despite what you've done, which I know you are sorry for, I'm a forgiving person. It's

Christmas. I believe in Christmas miracles. Deep down, Edrick is a forgiving person too. He's made that way."

Danica silently prayed for a Christmas miracle. She would take any fix to her and Edrick that she could get.

"Do you think he'll listen?" she asked.

"I think you care enough for him to make him listen and believe you as I have. Take a few minutes to gather yourself. Unpack all this luggage and join us in the main lobby where all the festivities are taking place. You'll recognize Edrick. He's the one in the red suit and shiny black belt. Are you up for it?"

"I do believe I am."

"Awesome! If he's not there, he'll be in Al's office getting ready."

"I will be there. Thanks for the talk and for listening to me. I was ready to leave it all here."

"Not with what the two of you have found together. Don't you leave here without knowing if there is a chance for you to have more. I want that for you and especially for him. I'll see you downstairs?"

Danica sniffled, feeling emotional. She's never had anyone in her corner like this. Not even the real, true friends she had back home.

"Yes. I will be there with Christmas bells on."

When Misha left, Danica grabbed her suit case, rummaged through it and found the Santa's helper, green wool dress with a black belt around it. She knew that Edrick had offered to play Santa. She had found a green dress in the resort shop and decided she would surprise him as his helper for the day. If he will have her, she still wanted to. She was counting on the real Santa to make her dream come true. She wanted her man back. There had been too many times in her life when she'd given up and threw in the towel. This would not be one of those times. Thanks to Misha's appearance, she had a renewed strength to change the image she had of Christmas. She'd found good in it again. She was making a vow to never let anything destroy the warmth and happiness of the holiday; never again.

Racing to her bedroom, she danced as she moved. She stopped in the doorway knowing she had left one thing behind. On the fireplace, she'd left a piece of mistletoe she'd purchased the day before. The impulsive purchase now had a use. She was full-in on the Christmas spirit. Now, she just needed Edrick.

12

Edrick was waiting in Albert's office until it was time to go into the lobby to take on his role as Santa Claus for the next few hours. Even though he was having a pity party, he had a job to do. There would be tons of kids looking for Santa to be happy and jolly. After getting the Santa suit on and stuffed until he barely recognized himself, he was glad he didn't let the plight of his current mood or his personal life interfere with putting smiles on kids' faces.

"You've never looked better. You could use a little workout, but other than that, I think you're ready, Santa. I see my team got you all dressed and ready. Is it hot in there?" Albert asked, poking at him in jest.

Edrick laughed when Albert lightly punched the fluff that made up the fat around his waist.

"Naw, it's not too bad. Besides, we're at a winter resort – it's all good. How many kids did you say are here today?"

"About forty, not counting the adult ones who want to act like they're still kids with wishes. We have enough toys for triple that number of kids. We wanted to be sure we had enough. A lot of the families that were already scheduled to be here have already had Christmas with their kids. They brought bags of toys with them or shopped when they got to Denver."

"Were you able to accommodate the ones that came in with me on the plane?"

"Oh, yeah. Trust me, everyone is going to have a Merry Christmas this year."

"Not everyone," Edrick replied and then looked away.

"I heard that. You know, you could have a happy Christmas if you would talk to Danica."

Edrick cut his eyes at Albert and sharply turned his head in the opposite direction.

"You can't be serious. After what she did?"

Edrick wasn't shy about the impact her deceit had no his psyche. He was still fiercely angry that her interest in him wasn't real; not even close to how his was for her. The fact that he sat up all night looking out at the snow-covered hills while also remembering the night before when he spent the best night of his life not just loving Danica, but having her in his arms while he slept, didn't escape him. That was the kind of peace he'd been looking for and didn't know it.

"You're in love with her. I know she did a wrong thing, but according to Misha, she really did try to fix it."

Edrick looked over in Al's direction as he adjusted

the belt around his waist. He tried not to show any real interest in Al hitting his truth on the head. He decided to let the "L" word live quietly in the air for the moment. He, too, had come to that realization in the night; not that it was a real surprise to him. His heart knew.

"Misha? What did she have to do with any of this? What does she know?"

Edrick was surprised to hear that Misha knew anything other than what he'd told them both. He should know that she and Al had no secrets between them. Al had to have brought her up to date on what happened in this very office the day before.

"She went to see Danica about an hour ago. She woke up this morning determined to rip into Danica. Before you get all hyper, their chat started out that way, but ended totally different."

Edrick was definitely interested now.

"Is that so?" he asked curiously. He knew how Misha could be. He only hoped Danica survived the tongue-lashing Misha was known to dish out.

"It is. She said they talked and Danica showed her emails between her and her office where, prior to you finding out about what she was up to, she had already messaged her office that she wasn't doing it. She told them that it wasn't in her to do the kind of story they wanted her to do on you. She refused. Even in the emails that she showed Misha, when they asked her if she had developed feelings for you, she didn't admit it.

She wanted to keep everything on a business level. She shared that it was wrong and that she was about to tell you all about it. Shortly after, you had that late lunch with us and she didn't want to ruin your fun when you went skiing. She was telling the truth when she said she was going to tell you."

"She told Misha all of that?"

Edrick was surprised. One, he was shocked that Misha would even go to see Danica. Then, he was flabbergasted that Danica would share the whole story with her since they'd only met earlier in the day. He shouldn't be surprised. He'd fallen for Danica within hours and in two days, he'd told her more about him than he'd shared with anyone in a long time.

"She did and Misha convinced her to stay. She was going to leave today. Did you know that? Before you answer, of course you didn't. You spent the remainder of yesterday in your room, alone. The only reason why you're not leaving tomorrow is because Misha would skin you alive. Man, look, I know what Danica did was bad. I'm with Misha; it's a forgivable offense. She didn't turn over anything about you; nothing. She not only told them she wouldn't do the task, way before you found out, but she quit her job even when they threatened to sue her for doing so, calling it a breach of the contract she signed. Her job was fully based on her outcomes. With this, to them, she failed miserably. To my relief, I'm glad she did. You should be too. They used her. You know how that industry is. They will use their own mothers to get a story. They played Danica because of her past, making her think she was lucky they were giving her a chance when no one else would. I haven't seen you as happy as you were with her in a lot of years. Do you really want to let her leave here without you trying to work it out?"

"Oh, you believe her too, huh?"

"Don't you? Think about the time the two of you shared. She couldn't make that up. She couldn't craft that stuff up. Do you think she's that type of conniving woman? Now that you've have a night to calm down from the height of the conversation yesterday, you should talk to her. Don't let her walk out of your life. Look how long it took you to find a woman who had you out here agreeing to be Santa? Santa Claus, bro! Santa! You hear me, right? Before you try to deny it, look at yourself. Look at how you're dressed. That's all I'm going to say."

Edrick didn't need to look at himself. He knew how he was dressed. The excitement that flowed through him as he got dressed did not go unnoticed. He couldn't wait to see the kids.

"I'm sure you have more, but I digress, just in case," he joked.

"You haven't smiled this much in years. You haven't skied in over four years. You were out here dancing and having a good time. She brought you back to life in her own way. It wasn't the way you would have chosen, but it worked."

Edrick knew every word coming out of Albert's mouth was true. The passion between he and Danica, the affection he felt between them, the comfort he had with her, he had never experienced that before. He was angry with Danica, but she hadn't followed through because she cared about him too much to hurt him like that. He hadn't said the words to Albert or Misha, but it was true that he was in love with Danica. The mere thought of it scared him. Who falls in love in a few hours? Clearly, he did. He didn't want her to leave. He wanted to give her a chance to tell him all she wanted to tell him before he stormed off the day before. Being alone the night before was a lesson learned for him. He didn't like the feeling. He didn't want to go back to closing himself off to the possibility that he could have a loving relationship again. He missed Danica so much the night before, he ached with the idea that they were going their separate ways. What she tried to do wasn't the way to go about getting a story, but he did admit that when he looked in her eyes in his anger, he saw love. He didn't see guilt over being caught. He saw guilt over knowing that he didn't deserve to be a target. She didn't deserve to be placed in the position she was in. His heart knew this was fixable. He had to do it.

"Do you think she'll want to talk to me after the things I said yesterday?" he asked Albert.

"Yes, I do."

Edrick turned his head toward the door where Danica stood in a green dress with a belt on that matched his. In her hand she held a green and white hat Christmas had with a big white bushy ball on the end which matched her dress.

Without caring about anything but seeing her and knowing that he could have lost her over what she never followed through on, he smiled. He wanted her to know that he missed her the night before. Last night didn't feel so right. It was all shades of wrong. Danica looked like an angel standing in the door waiting for his reaction. He needs her. He missed her. He wants her.

"This time I'm going to leave the two of you alone. Edrick, you've got about twenty minutes before forty screaming kids are going to be hollering where is Santa! Danica, it's good to see you."

When Albert passed by her, Danica grasped his arm lightly and leaned close to his ear.

"I'm sorry," she said.

"I know and it's okay. It's Christmas and it's a brand-new day."

Albert patted her on the shoulder.

Edrick wanted to stand, but he knew if he stood, with all of the extra weight on him, he may tumble over. He was still getting used to the suit.

"Hi," he said.

Danica smiled. The softness in his voice was back.

"Hi. I'm so sorry, Edrick. I really am. I don't know what I was thinking even agreeing to it. I didn't mean to hurt you in any way. I was going to leave because I thought you wouldn't want to see me."

Edrick exhaled and silently gave thanks that she hadn't left. Albert and Misha were both right. Her actions were forgivable. People make mistakes. He's made them and he knew that she had too. Why shouldn't he be forgiving? Seeing her standing there, he knew he already was.

"I'm sorry too for not letting you say your peace yesterday. It was a lonely night without you in my arms," he admitted.

"Whew, tell me about it. Never has my bed felt as cold as it did all night. I missed you."

"I missed you too. Merry Christmas."

When Danica smiled at him, he knew things were going to be alright between them. It will take some time, but he wanted to remain open to it. They had something special and he didn't want to let it go.

"Merry Christmas, Santa. You look nice in the suit. Can I come sit on Santa's lap and tell him about all the things I did wrong? I think he should hear the full story before he leaves coal under my tree," she said.

"Nope. Santa wants to move beyond it and let that be the past. It was just yesterday, yes, but today is a new day, just like Al just said. It's Christmas. I'm dressed as Santa and it looks like you're in the Christmas spirit as well, Mrs. Claus. You sure do look mighty nice in that short green dress. Why don't you come sit on Santa's lap and tell him what you would like for Christmas?"

Edrick patted his legs, winked and chuckled when Danica rushed over and planted herself square in the middle of his lap.

"Well, first, I need a job, Santa. I quit the last one because it wasn't for me. In fact, I'm thinking about a change in careers. Being a bad person and hurting others is not my cup of tea. I met a man who allowed me to see a reflection of the good person I am and want to continue being. Any suggestions?" she asked.

Danica's arms went around his neck and before he could speak, her lips touched his. The kiss was exactly what she needed. The way he was going at her lips told her that he felt the same way. She knew she was a lucky woman to be able to have him in her life after almost losing him.

"I'm Santa, so I know you're talented. You can get whatever job you want. Tell me what you have in mind and I'll make it happen. Santa Claus can bring about miracles. Look at us. We're miracles in the making."

"I love the sound of that. Can we miracle-make a little later?" she asked.

Edrick caught on and wiggled under her.

"I'm ready now!" he shouted, causing them to laugh together.

"But first, more kissing?"

Danica revealed the mistletoe she'd been holding in her other hand. She raised it above his head.

"Definitely more kissing. Hold on to that mistletoe. I have a headboard and some tape. It needs a permanent place while we're here so that we don't forget that there may have been a reason for the layover, but now, it's a purpose."

"I like the sound of that. I can feel your purpose. Can I make it up to you for all the hurt?" she whispered just before Edrick kissed her passionately again.

"How about Santa answers that later on. Y'all are nasty. What if a kid decided to walk by here and saw you all over Mrs. Claus with your hand planted squarely on her ass?" Misha quipped, entering the room. She raced over and pulled Danica from his lap. Edrick faked frowning.

"They would say, go Santa, it's your birthday!" he sang and pulled Danica back onto his lap.

"Looks like the two of you have talked and worked things out," Misha noted.

"No. We've decided to not go back and revisit that. I don't want to focus on the negative; not now and not while I'm dressed as Santa Claus, the happiest being living this time of year. It's over and done with. I want to move forward. We have things to work out, but I'm trusting my gut and my feelings," he said.

Edrick meant every word. He was glad they will have a chance to make it up to each other. He looked forward to hopefully not having another night like last night; a lonely one.

"Good. Be in your feelings later. You too, Mrs. Claus. Kids are waiting. If you don't get out there soon, I think they're going to start rioting. You have no idea how violent kiddies can get when there is a promise of Santa and he's in here getting a lap dance!" Misha joked.

Edrick laughed, and like jolly ol' Santa, his belly shook.

"Keep that in mind later too," he whispered to Danica before she stood.

Misha turned and left the office leaving them alone again.

Danica placed her hat on her head and turned in various directions to make sure she was presentable.

"I think I'm ready," she said.

"Shall we go make an appearance?" Edrick asked.

"Yes, we should."

"Don't forget the mistletoe for later."

Danica kept her eyes on him. She followed his gaze as she slipped the greenery down the front of her dress, making it disappear for now.

"You can get that later," she purred.

"Oh, I intend to."

"Can we shut ourselves away tonight? I know there are lots of events planned. I only want you."

Edrick pulled her into his arms as much as he could with the extra padding in front of him.

"I'm cooking us dinner. We'll pop some popcorn and watch Christmas movies. I have a gift for you."

"Mmm, I know you do."

"Well, yes, there is that, but I have an actual gift for you."

"Great minds think alike. I have one for you. I was going to leave it at the front desk."

"I'm glad you were on the plane. I know it's been a crazy few days with things going up and down and then all around. I want to see where this thing between us can go. Up for that?" he asked.

"For that and then some. Merry Christmas, baby."

Danica accepted the kiss and looked for more than she can stand by way of more kisses.

"Merry Christmas to you. Let's go do what we're dressed to do. Kids are waiting."

Danica took Edrick's hand. She loved Christmas again. After all, she was Mrs. Claus – how could she not.

Epilogue

Christmas
A Few Years Later

"Look at the big Christmas tree, Logan," Danica said, chasing behind her fast moving, almost three-year-old son. She, Edrick and Logan had just arrived at the resort in Denver two days before Christmas. To say they were excited to be back at the place where they first fell in love wouldn't describe the jovial experience. They would have been in Denver a few days earlier, but Edrick wanted to host a company-wide celebration for his employees at his New York City office. The moment the event was over, they boarded their private plane. On the plane ride Logan had been fussy and did the only thing he loved doing; he crawled into his daddy's lap and fell asleep. Sitting across from them, she watched them both sleep after Edrick strapped Logan in. They were her life. As Logan raced around giggling while dragging his favorite Minion toy around on the floor, she finally caught up to him as she checked out the extensive decorations she knew Misha had been working on for weeks.

Though this wasn't the first year they'd been back to Denver after that first Christmas, this time of year was special for them. Neither of them had ever again lost the Christmas spirit. Their love kept the holiday front and center in their lives.

Edrick was someplace gathering all of their luggage for the two-week stay they were planning. Logan had been fussy from the airport all the way to the resort until he saw the many holiday decorations. There was on thing about their son; he loved having his feet on the ground where he could run as fast as he could; that was his thing. He didn't like being strapped into a seat. She was surprised that at three, he knew his way around the resort and where to find everything. It wasn't his first time at the resort and would not be the last. In fact, in two days, not only would it be Christmas morning, but it would also be Logan's third birthday.

On the plane ride, she reminisced about how her life had changed for the better. There was a little bump in the road to their love, but nothing was going to keep them apart. She and Edrick were determined to love by any means necessary.

A year after she and Edrick first met, they were married at the resort the very next Christmas. All of her family attended along with family Edrick had that he'd lost touch with, but reconnected with. A few months later in April, they found out she was pregnant. True to how their lives went, Logan was born on Christmas Day in Chicago where they had traveled for Thanksgiving to spend with her family. When she was placed on bedrest, they stayed at a condo they owned in Downtown Chicago. As if their lives were being scripted, she went into labor on Christmas eve. Two hours into Christmas, Logan was born. Shortly after the first of the year, they headed to their home in Spain. She understood why Edrick loved Madrid so much; it had become one of her favorite places to be. Whenever they got the chance, she loved coming back to the States to visit everyone, especially Albert, Misha and their kids, which now consisted of their, not just their oldest son, but also a set of twins born a year ago.

With Logan headed for the tree's bright lights and decorations, out of nowhere came Albert. The minute Logan saw him, he changed course and ran straight for his godfather.

"My Logie! You're here!" Albert shouted, scooping Logan up in his arms. "Where's Edrick?" he added.

"Fooling with luggage. There is a lot of it since we'll be here for a few weeks, maybe longer."

"Longer sounds good. Misha will be happy to hear there you're here. She's been crazy all week running around getting things done with twins on her hips. Thankfully, she's planning to take the next few weeks off to just spend it with you. I even hired extra staff to cover her workload."

Danica walked over into Albert's outstretched

arms.

"I'm so happy to be here. It feels like forever since we were here last. What was it? June?" she asked, taking Logan from his arms when he began to fuss because he wanted to get down. She put him on the floor but kept him close.

"Yes, for the twins' party. We've been looking forward to you coming for Christmas. Before I forget, your brother is already here. He told me to tell you he was going skiing and would come by your suite in a few hours. He has thanked me a million times for giving him his own room this year. He said you promised him if he made the Dean's list at Howard University that you would give him some space this year."

Danica laughed out loud.

"I did make Mason that promise. I have found that if I promise him things based on how good his grades are, he comes through."

"Yeah, he said he's hitting you up next for the down payment on a car."

"He spends more of the money from my book royalties than I do."

She was an author. The idea of it all popped in her head. She said she wanted to get away from being a journalist, but she was happy to be a writer; her childhood dream. She was still pinching herself daily at the idea of the path her life had gone after she and Edrick left the resort that first year. It had been all good from that moment.

"That's what happens when you have the number one science fiction book in the country. The extra books for your book signing came in a few days ago. Misha had the event planner put up posters everywhere. Resort guests have been overwhelming us with messages about how they can get into the signing event."

"You told them it's free, right?" she asked.

"Definitely. There will barely be standing room. We're bringing other guests from other resorts. I know you were open to traveling to each one to do a signing, but that's a lot. We're going to set you up in the Crystal Room for New Year's Day. All of the resorts are completely booked and people are anxious to get their signed copy of your book. How did you come up with the title, *Korinth: They Live Among Us*? And when is the next book in the series coming out?"

Danica was happy that she had finally found her niche in life. She realized it was time to follow her dream and finally write her book. With its release six months ago, it still remained at the top spot on every bestseller list.

"I had that title in my head since, like, high school or college. I was sidetracked for a while, but once I left here that first year, I wanted to completely change my direction. While working on my relationship with Edrick, he helped me form a plan for my book. I didn't think a long-distance relationship could be so fulfilling."

"It was only long distance for a few months. Thanks to you, he moved to Chicago and started spending more time in the states. We played more golf in that first year of the two of you dating than I had with him in the four years or so before that. See, Christmas is magical in all kinds of ways."

"The magic is all Edrick!" she declared.

"Dada," Logan yelled. He knew his father's name.

"Ah, Mr. Magic himself," Albert said.

"He's my Mr. Magic! If it had not been for that layover at Christmas time a few years ago, I wouldn't be on the right track now. I owe a lot to you and Misha. I would have left here and walked away from my destiny. I'm glad I didn't."

"So am I. I'm going to go find him and see if I can help. Two weeks or more of being here with Logan and all the stuff you travel with, I know it's a lot. All the help we have here and he still insists on doing it all."

When Albert jogged toward the main entrance, Danica followed where Logan was taking her. She picked him up in her arms and walked him toward the big tree again.

"This is where mommy and daddy fell in love. We will spend every Christmas right here. This place changed my life. Out of that came you and I think a little brother or sister soon."

Danica giggled to herself hoping that her twice-missed cycle meant that she and Edrick were going to be parents again. They were hoping to have lots of children.

"Truck," Logan shouted and pointed.

Danica saw lots of truck ornaments on the tree, his second favorite kind of toy. She was happy that the toys for Logan for Christmas morning that Edrick sent ahead early were wrapped and by now, under the tree in their suite.

"I know you love trucks. Santa will bring you plenty of them. You know, in a few days, daddy will be sitting in the big ol' chair under the tree granting all kinds of Christmas wishes. They will all come true. How do I know? Because I wished for him and you, and Santa said yes."

When her wish for Edrick had come true, nothing else mattered. Not being sued by GBN News, their way of trying to hit her for not doing what they paid her to do. Just when she was ready to pay the suit off, she received notice that the lawsuit was withdrawn. It wasn't until she received an email from Hailey telling her that Edrick had used his pull, having worked with the owner of GBN to expand his investment portfolio, that she knew what real love meant. She thanked Edrick, though he reminded her that no thanks was necessary. He loved her and he wouldn't let anyone come for her. That started the beginning of their forever.

"Hey baby!" she heard Edrick calling to her.

As Logan turned and raced toward him, she followed suit. That Christmas layover brought her life to this. She would forever be grateful.

"Merry Christmas!" she responded going into his outstretched arms.

"Merry Christmas, my love!"

The Sullivans of Montana, Book 4
Three's a Crowd

Businessman Shelton Sullivan was clear that as a kid, he loved life growing up on the Sullivan Ranch wrangling cattle and riding horses. As a man, he prefers big city life, wrangling expensive suits and most of all, riding sexy women. He was blindsided when a woman penetrated the wall of steel that surrounded, what some said was his black heart, when it came to being in love; he preferred lust.

Deputy Sheriff McKenna Gibson needed a fresh start in a new city. Escaping a life that was crafted for her had become old and dull. Sizzling, spicy encounters with Bozeman's most eligible bachelor was exactly what she needed to help her forget the secrets she was hoping to leave behind in her old life as a military wife.

Without warning, Shelton found himself swept up into McKenna's amorous sensualities that very much matched his own dalliances. Their steamy, seductive encounters led to even more explicit and erotic romps until Shelton's world crashed down like a Montana boulder. McKenna is injured in the line of duty and his world is rocked off of its axis when her military husband blew up the love he thought was blossoming from the one time he decided to let down his guard.

Is Shelton willing to forgive and forget and turn away from the red hot stirring in his chest at the thought of her?

Get Shelton and McKenna's story, Three's a Crowd, the fourth book in the Sullivans of Montana series. It's available now for preorder at

www.cherylbarton.net
and www.amazon.com/author/cherylbarton

An Unexpected Destiny
Sister Act Series, Book 1

Now available!

Destiny Lockhart's high school crush, Lincoln Cole, is again front and center in her life. She last saw him fifteen years ago when she threw him out of her bedroom after their one night together following the senior prom. That night had been her most embarrassing moment, leaving her feeling ashamed and undesirable.

There was no way entertainment mogul Lincoln Cole could ever forget the shy, yet beautiful butterfly that was Destiny from his years as a high school football star. The now feisty, sexy and self-confident executive who dripped in vibrant, dazzling appeal reminded him that they were never meant to only have a one-night-stand. They were always destined for forever.

For years, they lived on two different coasts unaware that soon, their past would become an unexpected present filled with unfinished desires that once looked like rejection.

Get your copy now!

If you enjoyed, *An Unexpected Destiny*, book one of the "Sister Act Series" you are going to love book 2,

For You I Will

Kasey Young discovered that a man would do anything to keep her in his grips, even if it's her ex-husband. She lived her life his way for years until she'd had enough and filed for divorce. He wants to insert himself back into her life with an ultimatum; take him back or lose custody of their kids. Kasey found herself between a rock and a hard place needing the help of a man she barely knew, but who stirred up deep carnal desires that had been lying dormant.

Attorney Darren Braxton stepped up to the plate to help Kasey with her child custody case as a favor for a friend. What he hadn't planned on was the hedonistic lust for a woman who could cause him to lose all he's gained because he can't say no to her. He did the one thing he could think of to save them both; he married her.

Kasey has to convince the court that their love is real or she could lose everything. Could she before it's too late?

"Preorder your copy of For You I Will" on February 14, 2022 for this August 2022 release

It Should Have Been You

Available now on Kindle Unlimited – read for FREE!
www.cherylbarton.net

Karma:
Dr. Clayton Myers was never a believer in karma, but he did believe in fate. Both would soon collide and expose a secret that would impact the perfect life and relationship with the only woman he ever loved, but not the only woman he took to his bed. That revelation would put his life on a path he accepted while never forgetting what could have been.

Disappointment:
Dr. Donna Spencer had experienced one of the darkest days of her life at the hands of the man who made a promise of forever. She took the hit to her heart and realized nothing good lasts forever.

Fate:
After years of no contact, Clayton and Donna's paths would cross again, forcing them to face the past where their love resided, while wondering what should have been and if they could find their way back to love again.

The Power of Seduction

Bakery owner Raquel Hastings assumed her relationship was perfect in every way, both in and out of the bedroom where she had enjoyed the most tempting, titillating, and out-of-this-world sensual romps between the sheets with sexy engineer, Preston Sharpe, a man who knows his way around a woman's body. That was until he took a job in another country which left her only with memories and intoxicating desires to be loved like that again. Her world had been turned upside down until the day he returned with a plan to turn her world right side up.

Preston's alluring visions of Raquel haunted him at night, alone in his bed in a foreign country without the woman he loved. With the chance to return home and to her loving arms, he dreamed of once again sharing nights of satiating passion that only two hearts meant for each other could share. He knew he had to ready his game of seduction if he were ever going to again have Raquel back in his life and in his bed. This time, his plan was to make it last forever with the hope that Raquel could forgive him and give their love another chance.

Read it for free on Kindle Unlimited!

Make sure you check out book 1, of "The Brothers of Chi-Town", *I Can't Let Go* – now available for download and in paperback.

I Can't Let Go

Carter Garrison vowed to love, honor and cherish his wife, Sienna, forsaking all others, something he forgot to do during a weekend of fun, bad company and poor judgement.

Sienna Garrison never dreamed her college sweetheart, Carter, whom she pledged her life to, would break her heart and when he did, she moved out and moved on - or tried to.

What better occasion is there than a friend's wedding to stir up old feelings and memories of love, intense passion and nights of sensual titillation. Gazes from across a room after almost two years apart revealed depths of love that had never died.

Seeing Sienna again reminded Carter of what he'd lost and he vowed to never let go by doing whatever he could to get his wife back even if it included begging and pleading. Is Sienna ready to forgive and take a chance on life again with the only man she'd ever really loved?

When Carter brings on the charm and turns up the heat, no woman is immune, especially Sienna.

Don't forget to snag your copy of book 2,
Swagger and Baggage, in "The Brothers of Chi-
Town" series – now available

Swagger and Baggage

It's not a coincidence that casino owner, Torrence Allen, ran into his college sweetheart, Reese Michaels again; it's fate. As his memories unfold, he had tried everything to keep her in his life and his bed back then and failed at both. She wasn't ready for him then, but he hopes she is ready for him now.

Reese Michaels never thought she'd see Torrence again. Their split in college was dramatic and hurtful and still, no man had been able to win her heart. She considered herself the permanent third wheel to friends who had found love and marriage.

Torrence's swagger has always won women over, but it's his baggage that's causing his life to spiral out of control. He messed up and found himself without the woman he has always loved.

About the Author

Cheryl Barton lives in Maryland and in her spare time she loves to read espionage, crime, and romance novels, cook, watch Sci-fi movies, craft, spend time with family and friends, and enjoy Maryland steamed crabs. In 2018, Cheryl celebrated 30 years as a government employee and loves writing romance and inspirational novels during her downtime.

Cheryl is the author of multiple romance and inspirational novels and is proud of 4 book compilation projects with several other incredible women called, "One Sister Away: Encouraging Words from One Sister to Another" – a series of books meant to encourage, empower and inspire other women. People often ask Cheryl which book is her favorite of all of those she's written. While she finds it hard to select one favorite, Cheryl still looks to her first novel, Bachelor Not for Sale, if she had to pick a favorite because it was her first novel and the one that inspired her to continue writing.

In 2014 & 2016, at the 5th and 7th years of the African American Author's Expo, Cheryl was recognized for her work as an accomplished published author, receiving a certificate and award for both years.

Cheryl was a 2018 Finalist of the Literary Trailblazer of the Year award, given by the Indie Author Legacy Awards' yearly event.

Cheryl was a 2019 Finalist for the Emma Award

given by Romance Slam Jam and a 2018 Finalist for the Literary Trailblazer of the Year award by the Indie Author Legacy Award. Cheryl is a member of the Contemporary Romance Writers where she currently serves on the board as the secretary.

Connect with Cheryl at:

Website:
https://www.cherylbarton.net

Facebook
https://www.facebook.com/authorcherylbarton/

Twitter
https://twitter.com/CBartonBooks

Instagram
https://www.instagram.com/cherylbartonbooks/

Pinterest
https://www.pinterest.com/crbarton30/

YouTube
https://youtu.be/7u3DxfgN61s

Amazon Page
https://www.amazon.com/author/cherylbarton

Book Bub
https://www.bookbub.com/authors/cheryl-barton

www.ingramcontent.com/pod-product-compliance
Lightning Source LLC
Chambersburg PA
CBHW050841180626
46814CB00007B/2571